Praise for Jack & Diane

"OMG! I read this in 6 hours! James Weaver writes like the movie "The Christmas Story" and had me laughing out loud and crying real tears." – *Amazon Review*

"I couldn't put this book down. Reading it brought back memories and stirred emotions that stayed with me well after I was finished. Take the time to get to know Jack and Diane. You won't be disappointed!" – *Amazon Review*

"The best thing about Weaver's book is its often elegant, lovely prose, along with an opening scene that draws the reader in immediately. His book is quite charming, with characters who are fully-drawn and believable. I'm almost exactly of the right age to read this book, having lived through the time, with all of its music and cultural references. But even readers who are younger and older than me will enjoy the book, because the book's power is not in its cultural specificity, but in its characters." – *Writer's Digest Self-Published Book Awards Judge*

"A beautiful coming of age story." – *Goodreads Review*

"I couldn't put this down from page one. I think we can all relate to these characters and relive our youth again. It was beautiful and heartbreaking." – *Amazon Review*

"Loved it! Totally didn't see the end coming...such a good book!" – *Goodreads Review*

"A very emotional walk through life that just about anyone can relate to. I highly recommend it!" – *Amazon Review*

"I laughed, cried, gasped, and recalled my youth as I read this truly touching story of love. A refreshing story in the times we live in." – *Amazon Review*

JACK &
DIANE

ALSO BY JAMES L. WEAVER

Poor Boy Road

Ares Road

Blackbird Road

Asylum Road

JACK & DIANE

BY JAMES L. WEAVER

Book cover design by Don Browers

Acknowledgments

For Becky, Madison and Max from whom all good things flow. You are my daily inspiration. I love you guys more than I can express.

For Mom, who taught me to be generous and gentle and that I could be anything I wanted to be.

For Dad, who has always been my hero, who taught me the value of hard work and that life is a matter of priorities.

For my friends who read this work over the years and provided such great feedback, always encouraging and keeping me grounded: Donna Lite, my Devil's Advocate; Becky Howard, Devourer of Literature; and fellow author Barry Brakeville, who inspired me to pick the pen back up and just write. If I forgot anyone, my humblest of apologies.

For Don Browers for his excellent design work on the cover that captured the essence of the book in a glance. Thanks, Don.

CHAPTER ONE

I held my bleeding knuckles in my mouth, hunkering in an unyielding oak chair while awaiting my fate like some convicted criminal minutes from the march to his execution. The only things missing were an ancient priest in a long, black frock and a fellow convict in a dingy, grey tattered uniform rolling a rickety cart carrying my last supper.

Atop the scarred wood of the desk in front of me was a Newton's Cradle office trinket where silver balls clacked back and forth in an unending swing, the steel balls matching the ones knotting in my stomach. My vision shimmered as immense emotion replaced the unquenchable fury raging through me minutes before leaving my head throbbing and hands shaky. I swallowed hard to combat the overwhelming stench of Lysol and Principal Smithers' daily dousing of Old Spice, the offending scents hanging in the air like a poisonous cloud and pushing me toward the desire to hurl my lunch over the tidy desk.

The stories of those who sat in this very chair were stuff of legend. Even at the tender age of nine, I was smart enough to know while legends were great exaggerations of fact, there was always some smidgeon of truth. I knew I was in deep trouble, but how far the abyss extended remained to be seen.

As I stared at my distorted reflection in the steel balls, phones rang and typewriters clacked in the office behind me. Ms. Woodstone, the office warden, made calls to the people I least wanted to find out about this situation. Her low, gravelly voice sounded as if she started smoking in the womb. I hoped to God she talked to my mother. If they forced my father to leave work and drive across town, whatever fate Principal Smithers would deal me would be child's play compared to my father's wrath.

I swiveled at the soft, timid knock on the door behind me. Diane leaned against the frame with a tissue clamped against her nose, splotches of crimson dotting the tissue like polka dots. She'd pulled back her silky, raven black hair in a ponytail, revealing the splendor of her cherubic face. Though facing certain death for my playground crimes, my spirits lifted at the mere sight of her. She gazed at me for a moment, hypnotizing me with her icy blue eyes. She could have told me to stab myself in the leg with a letter opener, and I would have done it without a second thought.

"Why'd you punch Jimmy?" she asked at last, head cocked at an angle, removing the tissue from her nose.

I shifted my eyes to the floor and shrugged. "I don't know."

I knew why, but I couldn't bring myself to tell her. I left my bravado on the playground imbedded in the crumpled form of Jimmy Galdano. My controversial move ran counter to the unwritten dodge ball rule that whoever stepped to the wall was fair game. If someone knocked your block off, it was your own fault for not getting out of the way. But, the malevolence in Jimmy's squinty, narrow eyes as he honed in on Diane as his target set me off. While the bloodthirsty blacktop horde of grade

2

schoolers cheered him for his accuracy, I shoved my fist down his pudgy throat. I beat Jimmy like a shady loan shark would a delinquent client, ignorant of the cheering crowd or my bloodied knuckles. I don't even remember the teacher pulling me off, my vision and senses clouded in a haze of rage.

I did have an answer to her question, but there wasn't a snowball's chance in hell I could muster the courage to tell her. And tell her what? That she consumed my thoughts nearly every waking moment? How it took the summation of my willpower to resist reaching forth and stroking those dark curls as I sat behind her in class? I couldn't say any of it without sounding like a psycho stalker. Instead, I clamped my lips together and pumped my shoulders.

"Well," she said, a coy smile blooming as the nurse arrived at her side to take her back to class. "Thank you, Jack. I liked it."

As they walked down the hall and out of view, her angelic image floated in front of me, the simple act of her mentioning my name lifting my spirits and soul in a way nothing else could, or ever would. She may as well have been wearing a halo. When Principal Smithers's pear frame filled the door, his bulbous lips clamped together with such force they disappeared altogether, I realized nothing could penetrate the impervious armor provided by Diane's beaming face.

CHAPTER TWO

The human mind is an amazing contraption. I can't
remember where I put my car keys five minutes ago or what I
ate for lunch yesterday, but the moment I first laid eyes on Diane
Riven will be forever etched in my mind. I planted my feet by the
mailbox outside of my house in Shawnee, a middle-class suburb
of Kansas City. Tidy Colonial homes spread across the narrow
street lined by trees that spit their gargantuan burnt orange leaves
to the ground as summer gave way to fall.

Like a caged tiger, I'd paced across my father's prized
grass in my front yard watching prospective buyers tour the
empty house across the street, tossing a scuffed baseball in the air
and catching it without looking in my well-oiled mitt. The house
once contained my best friend in the world, Bobby Turner, who
moved to the barren wastelands of Colorado. I had no idea if
Colorado was barren, but I had to assume Bobby was trapped in
a place whose terrain was as miserable as I felt.

After Bobby moved away, I moped around the house,
head hung low, beseeching pity from anyone who would bestow it
upon me. It was an effective strategy in the short term, but wore
razor thin with my parents after a couple of weeks. My sadist
teenage brother Jake cut me zero slack from the moment Bobby's

moving van pulled out of the driveway.

"Grow up, you moron," he said, shoving me into the wall as he passed my sulking mug. "Christ, you'd think you were married to him."

My brother—the epitome of compassion. He was mad because I snapped a Polaroid of him in his underwear trying to dance like John Travolta from Saturday Night Fever while singing the Bee Gees. Believe me, I wish my young eyes were never exposed to such an atrocity, but I held the picture as ransom to save me from future wet willies and red bellies.

Bobby's house remained empty for several months, and I manned my post by our mailbox like a dutiful soldier, scrutinizing each potential buyer, making an immediate determination on whether or not they'd make suitable neighbors, and praying accordingly for their return or demise. I longed for the Turner station wagon with its smoking muffler and wood grain paneled doors to wheel back into the driveway. Of course, like most things we wish for, it didn't happen.

Imagine my dismay, when I returned from the movies one Saturday and found cars parked in the Turner's driveway with boxes and toys splayed in the grass like they hosted a yard sale. My spirits, bolstered by the wondrous world of light sabers, X-wings and Darth Vader from Star Wars, now sunk to an all-time low. Reality hit me like a right cross. Bobby Turner wouldn't live there again.

I scoped out the house for three tortuous days, hoping for a glimpse of the schmuck who took his place. The brisk October wind blew my brown hair across my hazel eyes, but didn't impede the vision before me. The moment her angelic face crossed the plane of her front door, time ground to a halt

Dressed in blue jeans and a white button-down, she stopped outside the screen door, surveying the steel gray line of clouds hooking to the east before taking several tentative steps to the brick walkway running alongside her white-faced home. Tight black curls blew across her porcelain face as cobalt blue eyes squinted against the wind. She caught me gawking, and my heart fluttered.

My jaw flapped open, chin resting on my heaving chest like an idiot, masses of falling leaves gathering in my gaping mouth—Jack Phipps, the human rake. She smiled and waved, and my heart exploded, hot blood spilling across my innards, weakening my knees. She stood there for an eternity, hand frozen in mid-air, waiting for me to do something. My mind raced at a numbing pace, thousands of potential responses crashing my brain, but none seemed appropriate to express the strange emotions swarming my system at the appearance of this beautiful stranger. Lacking anything appropriate to say, I did the one thing that came naturally—nothing. I left her hand hanging and ran back into my house like a big, fat coward.

I lingered at the living room window, peeking around the god-awful orange velour curtains my mother hung last week, hoping she wouldn't catch me watching. With her eyes locked on my house, she slumped her shoulders. Even from across the street, I spotted the tears welling in her baby blue eyes and I felt like the biggest piece of walking garbage to ever traverse the planet. She turned and disappeared into her house. It was 1977.

CHAPTER THREE

It took the defense of her honor to give me the courage to speak to Diane for the first time. We'd lived across the street from each other for weeks and my desk parked behind hers in school, but I was too much a coward to make the first move. However, in taking care of Jimmy Galdano, I shattered the barrier of cowardice I'd placed between us and we became quite the pair. Everyone thought it was great, except her father. My charms were lost on the man who, if he bothered to acknowledge my existence at all, would cast this malevolent glare like I'd walked through a steaming pile of dog crap and tracked it through his living room.

To say Diane's father didn't like me would be an extreme understatement. The man was a bean pole, so skinny he could wriggle his way through a keyhole. His pointy, bald head and rat-like, black eyes scared the bejesus out of me. He wore white, button-down dress shirts and slacks, as if wearing jeans or shorts were beneath him, and he smelled like he bathed in Listerine. He'd hunch in his oversized recliner as he read the newspaper, eyeballing me over the top of the page with narrowed, dark eyes like a vulture waiting for its prey to gasp a last breath. He apparently perceived something unsettling in the way I looked at his only daughter. It took three years before he said more than five words to me.

Diane's parents were the antithesis of what I envisioned as your standard American married couple. The couples my parents hung out with were jovial, loving people. Each man and woman custom made for each other, one's strength binding the other's weakness. But, as much as these people seemed destined for each other, Diane's parents seemed polarized by our Creator to repel each other. Mrs. Riven was a beautiful woman with long, jet black hair, high cheekbones, a sharp nose and radiant blue eyes who smelled of lavender. It was as if the proverbial prom queen married the geeky president of the chess club.

I wasn't some poster child of the world's greatest kid, but I was well-liked in the parental circles and Mr. Riven's hatred of every fiber of my existence bothered the hell out of me. I wondered if I imagined things so I decided to ask my father. His level of brutal honesty was legendary, though sometimes painful. If anyone would give me the skinny on Mr. Riven, it would be him.

My dad was a proud man who'd grown up dirt poor in central Nebraska. He'd worked hard all his life, earning each penny with blood and sweat. Nobody handed him anything and he expected nothing for free. I heard the phrase "In this life you get what you earn" more times than I care to remember, usually when I stuck out my empty palm asking for money.

My dad and Mr. Riven were nothing more than cordial to each other, a definite discomfort in their dialogue like two people out on a bad blind date. I asked him about it one day as we walked our street, his calloused hand resting on my bony shoulder as I kicked pinecones across the pavement.

"Do you like Mr. Riven, Dad?"

"Oh, not particularly," my dad said after a momentary pause, running his hand through his thick dark hair, now peppered with gray. He was a handsome man, though a decent pot-belly began to form on his six-foot-two frame. He still hit the weights and sported forearms like slabs of granite.

"Not particularly? What does that mean?"

"Well, it means I won't be hanging out with him on Sundays to watch the Chiefs or invite him to poker, but if he was on fire, I'd roll him on the ground to douse the flames and call the ambulance."

He wouldn't say any more on the subject no matter how hard I pressed him. I didn't like Mr. Riven one bit, but I wanted confirmation I wasn't out in left field. At the time, I took my dad's character judgment in hand and went with it. His disdain for the man at least confirmed my sanity. It wasn't until much later in life that I came to realize why my dad didn't like Mr. Riven.

Growing up, Jake and I never claimed to be bored–at least more than once. The last time we did, we spent three hours in the scorching July sun, moving a pile of landscaping rocks from one side of the driveway to the other with a couple of splintered, duct-taped shovels. There wasn't a particular reason why the rocks had to be moved. It was my father's way of squelching future complaints of boredom. Needless to say, neither Jake nor I burned with desire to find out what other tasks my father could conjure for us so we sought our own entertainment.

In contrast, I couldn't picture Mr. Riven moving a pile of rocks in the hot sun. When he did work in the yard, he covered himself head-to-toe as if he feared any exposure to the sun would result in instantaneous skin lesions. He contracted out any heavy labor and then tortured the contractors with his sharp tongue. My dad would rather have his fingernails pulled out with pliers than pay someone to do nothing more than exert a little sweat. Given their divergent ideologies, it was no wonder they didn't get along.

My mom and Mrs. Riven, on the other hand, got along like twin sisters. They were tentative at first, but after a matter of minutes alone in the kitchen, they laughed like they'd known each other for years. They were both homemakers and became fast friends over many morning coffees as they traded stories of their similar childhoods. So similar, one could make an argument they came from the same womb.

Diane and I made it through our awkward start, the emotions coursing through my psyche back then were nothing short of astounding. My level of comfort with her was like nothing I ever experienced, nor will ever expect to again. Though at nine I lacked the life experience to interpret these odd sensations, I knew there was something exceptional about that little girl.

During the late fall and winter months, we played outside, building snow forts and getting pelted with ice balls from my older brother and his delinquent friends. My brother's torture of me brought Diane and I closer together. She was a nurturer, a helper, one who came to the aid of those in need. It was a character trait which would serve her well in her future years, but would also serve as a great source of frustration for me throughout our relationship. She would try to pick up the broken pieces of other people's doomed relationships despite my fervent pleadings for her to stay out of it.

School passed through the winter and into the spring. Though unspoken by either of us, the other kids could tell we were "going together." We were joined at the hip most of the time, managing to find enough gender-neutral things to do so both of us could participate. That said, we still kept our own circle of friends. I didn't ask her to play football, and she didn't ask me to do whatever girls did at that age.

My parents were elated I found someone to replace Bobby. My mom thought little Diane was "just a peach." Mrs. Riven spoiled me with the royal treatment and her ever present mission to fatten me with cakes and cookies. Mr. Riven, however, remained reserved and aloof, saving his judgement for the inevitable moment when I would screw up and he could point to his unnerving ability to judge someone's character by their appearance. His disapproval of our time together was evident with each bone grinding handshake and vigilant eagle eyes scrutinizing my every move. Mr. Riven treated me like I was a flea-ridden mutt when I crossed the threshold of his home.

Spring rolled into summer and it came time for me to head north to Nebraska to spend the lion's portion of the summer on my Uncle Will's farm "building character." For the first time in my young life, there wasn't an ounce of excitement in my bones over my annual trip to my father's childhood home. As I packed my suitcase, I wore the varnish from the hardwoods in my bedroom spying out the window to catch a glimpse of Diane at the window in her room. After putting my suitcase in the trunk of my dad's boat of a Buick, I gazed one last time across the street, hoping Diane would see me off.

My dad tried to bustle us into the car to beat rush hour traffic out of town. I held my arm up and waved at my angel in the window. Diane stood unmoving, stone-faced in her blue floral dress, her long dark hair pulled back into a ponytail. As if sensing my need for some sort of acknowledgement, she returned my wave with a solitary flick of the wrist before moving to the interior of the house, expressing her disappointment of my two-month leave of absence. I waited a moment longer before climbing into the cavernous backseat of the Buick where you could sit five of your closest friends side by side without touching so much as an elbow. I remained silent most of the trip, unable to shake the image of her at the window.

CHAPTER FOUR

There's nothing quite like the overpowering bouquet of manure and the incessant metallic banging of hog bins to wake you from a peaceful slumber. The combined sensations could turn the mood of even the most cheerful of city-boys-at-heart foul. No matter how deep I dived under the patchwork quilt covering my bed, the aroma of cattle feces rolled its way across the clearing from the feed lot across the road, climbed the ivy running alongside my aunt and uncle's non-air-conditioned farmhouse and found me through my open window. The open window was a pure Catch-22 situation. If I left the windows closed, the summer night's heat would accumulate and I worried about bursting into flames. If left open, the manure aroma would destroy any chance of going back to sleep. Uncle Will laughed at my complaint over breakfast.

"Leave 'em open, boy," he said. "That's the smell of money."

I shook my head over my oatmeal. If shit was the smell of money, I'd rather die a pauper.

The farm consisted of a compact, white, two-story house built in the 1930's with peeling lead-based paint. It had six rooms and a solitary bathroom with an old claw foot tub rather than a shower. A weathered red barn slumped in the distance, its peeling front crowded with tractors and combines in various states of workability, and a boneyard of parts and equipment my uncle would never use, but couldn't get rid of "just in case." A large diesel fuel tank nestled in the shade of the barn with enough stained soil around it to raise the hairs of even the heartiest of EPA inspectors. A couple of iron pens hugged the barns where a gathering of noisy hogs slopped up the day's grub. Behind the barn ran the acres of corn and soy bean fields my uncle farmed, just as his father and grandfather had done. I haven't been back there for years, but I can envision it as clear today as ever.

The monotony of the farm was like having to watch the same movie on a loop, and for the first time I wasn't enjoying my stay. It used to be fun to toss feed to the chickens, to dump slop to the hogs or groom the horses in the barn. I used to love the howling winds of the central plains and the thousands of stars blanketing the night sky. But, this summer, Diane and the time I could be spending with her consumed my thoughts. My aunt and uncle were childless, and the only kids to play with were my brother and a neighbor kid his age named Randy who lived a half-mile down the gravel road. But, "play" wasn't the word I would use to describe their extracurricular activities. Slow torture would be more accurate.

They named their favorite activity the Jack Toss – a lovely little game consisting of grabbing me by one arm and foot, and spinning me around at the speed of light until I cried I would puke. They'd toss me into the pile of straw and manure accumulated from my cleaning of the horse stalls. While great fun for them, it became a source of great anxiety for me. I kept my head on a swivel, waiting for them to pounce when I tended to my duties. Uncle Will would chastise them, but deep down he thought it was funny since my father did the same to him when they were kids.

To my brother's detriment, however, I got older and craftier. I took his abuse because he dwarfed me in both height and breadth, but I managed to squeeze in my own measures of retribution.

One particular evening as I tracked the shadows on my bedroom wall, the window to Jake's room screeched open. I crawled out of bed and watched his shadow slink its way to the backside of the barn along with a person I assumed was Randy, the beams from their flashlights bouncing off the narrow dirt road leading to a creek running through my uncle's land. They went there to drool over old Playboy's by the light of an old kerosene lantern and smoke cigarettes lifted from my Uncle Will. The one time I drew enough courage to venture to the make-shift shack they'd built last summer, Jake kicked the crap out of me and threw me into the cold creek. I thought I would die of hypothermia.

After brief consideration, I decided against following them. For one thing, the narrow dirt path terrified me, and the sounds emanating from the forest sounded like some hideous ghoul lurking in the shadows waiting to suck the marrow from my bones. For another, if Jake and Randy caught me, they'd gag me, tie me to a tree and leave me out there for the wolves. As brave a person as I might portray, when it came to darkness I was such a chicken I'd lay money I could shoot an egg out of my butt given the right circumstances.

I waited in bed and tried to stay awake until they came back. After an hour, the sandbags over my eyelids slammed shut, and I fell into a nightmare where ghouls chased me through an ominous forest. Jake and Randy perched high in the trees cheering on the monsters.

In the next room, the sudden thud of body meeting floor snapped me out of the nightmare and I stifled a scream. Crawling out of bed, I crept to Jake's room and found his beer-reeking frame passed out on the hardwood floor, his bony arm reaching for the safety of the mattress. A wry, devious grin crossed my lips as I realized my means of revenge.

I settled at my bedroom window for hours, waiting for the first crack of light signaling daybreak. Once the sun poked its way over the lush, green horizon of waving cornstalks, the forest ghouls would slink back into the shadows, and I would be able to make my way to Jake and Randy's hideout unharmed to bring back evidence of their delinquency.

I was rather proud of myself as I made my way toward the barn. The warming rays of the sun shed their light on the fertile Nebraska land. The thick and heavy air signaled today would be a scorcher. Uncle Will's horses neighed a greeting to me as I passed their way, but I shushed them, feeding them carrots to buy their silence. Once I made it past the familiarity of the barn, my progress slowed due to the lingering darkness and my fear of the woods. Spitting out a quick prayer, I traversed the dirt pathway leading to Jake's hideout.

It took a few minutes to reach the shabby, wood clubhouse, but it seemed like an hour as the sounds of the wild woods amplified ten-fold. A cracking twig sounded like a gunshot, and the chirps of a bird like a shrieking banshee. Inside the shack, the reason Jake fell through the window and passed out on the floor lay before me. A full twelve-pack of empty Budweiser cans lay strewn on the dirt floor with a stack of dirty magazines scattered across an old tree stump serving as a coffee table.

I pulled out the backpack I brought and stuffed the empties into it, careful to dump any remnants of the beverage left in the cans. I batted away the angel on my shoulder as she whispered in my ear to abort my plan to spoil at least a portion of Jake's summer. Uncle Will was pretty open-minded, but he wouldn't be happy with his thirteen-year-old nephew guzzling his beer.

I made it back inside the farmhouse without a sound and slinked into Jake's room where he snored in resounding style, unaware of the shit storm I orchestrated. With the care of a surgeon, I placed the empty cans on the bed and on the floor. I was even brave enough to place one in Jake's grimy, open hand. The rooster's crow marked the seconds I had to make it back to my bed before Uncle Will clomped upstairs to rouse us for our morning chores.

Diving under the covers, I tried my best to feign sleep and not appear like the cat who swallowed the canary, but it was hard to keep a grin off my face. Uncle Will's heavy footsteps pounded on the hardwood downstairs, growing louder as they ascended to our floor. Jake's room was the first he would come to, and I held my breath lest I miss Uncle Will's reaction. The suspense killed me.

"What in the hell?" Uncle Will said, the volume of his voice growing as he flipped from stupefied to enraged. "Jake, get your ass up!"

Now my smile broke free from its thin-walled prison, and my cheeks ached from its magnitude. For the first time that summer, I enjoyed myself and Diane wasn't on my mind.

Jake's troubles with his drinking escapade were boundless, starting with a tortuous hour-long lecture from my father over the phone. My Uncle Will worked Jake like a dog, making him do everything and anything under the sun, sweating beer out of his system. To speed the process along, it was one of the hottest afternoons in recorded history without a trace of a breeze. The spectacle of Jake's skinny, sweat soaked body wearing an expression of sad, hungover misery on his face was one of the greatest visions I think I'll ever live to see.

As for retribution for my set up, none came. I thought Jake had enough brain cells to realize he didn't drag an empty twelve pack of cans back to his bedroom, but lucky for me he didn't make the connection. While I took frequent breaks sipping ice-cold lemonade in the shade with Uncle Will, we laughed at my older brother as he lifted heavy sacks of grain and dragged massive bales of hay. I think Jake was too sick to even get jealous.

I thought of Diane during those last few weeks, but far from the consuming frequency when I first arrived at the farm. I could still feel her hand in mine on the swing set in her backyard, and the mere thought of her still brought a healthy smile to my young face, but I wasn't obsessed.

Her letter arrived three days before my dad came to take us back to Kansas City. I recognized Diane's pinched writing style. Aunt Kate handed me the envelope, and I bolted to my room. Plopping on the bed, I stared at the envelope for several minutes, afraid to open it for some absurd reason. I raised it to my nose and inhaled as I'd seen in the movies, half expecting the scent of perfume. I tore the seal and extracted the folded piece of Big Chief tablet paper.

Dear Jack,
How are you? I am fine. It's been a boring summer here without you. I hope you had fun on the farm. Do they have chickens?

I guess you can tell me when you get home. Your mom said it would be soon. I think she is tired of me going over to your house to see if she knew when you would be home. I just wanted to tell you I can't wait to see you.

My heart pounded as I read those last few lines. My eye caught how she signed it—*Love, Diane*. Love, Diane. My enduring fear, unrealized until that moment, was she would forget me over the course of the summer. I would get back home and she would be hanging out in the backyard with Jimmy Young, shock exploding on her face as I opened the back gate.

"What the hell are you grinning about?" my brother asked from the doorway of my room. He scowled, the only way he ever looked at me, picking at a zit the size of a Buick on his forehead.

"Not a thing, Jake," I said with the letter in my tight grasp.

"Dumbass," he said, wiping pus on the doorframe as he left.

Images of Diane flooded my brain, my extremities tingling with this intense contentment and longing to be with her. If I thought my legs would carry me, I would have run all the way back home to Kansas.

CHAPTER FIVE

As we pulled into my driveway, Diane perched on her front step twirling a yo-yo in tiny loops. She wore the same blue flower dress she'd worn the day I left for the farm. I almost gave myself whiplash as we turned the corner, the immediacy of my desire to be with her overwhelming. She flashed her teeth and threw an exaggerated wave my way, but remained anchored to the step knowing a motherly assault loomed.

"Welcome home, boys," my mother said, swallowing us with a hug and kisses. She'd chopped her once long, silky brown hair, accentuating her chestnut eyes. Her petite frame exuded extraordinary strength as it gripped us, and I wondered if she'd been hitting Jake's weight set in the basement. "How was it?"

"It was okay," Jake mumbled, as if the question irritated him. I would adopt the same demeanor in a couple of years. It couldn't be helped. I think sullen irritation with the world is wired into a teenager's DNA. I returned my mother's hug and weathered through an onslaught of her sloppy wet kisses on my cheek, trying to restrain myself from peeking over my shoulder at Diane. I wanted my mother to think I was happy to see her.

"Oh, I missed you guys," she said, ruffling my thick

brown hair and squatting in front of me. "What did you do all summer?"

"Geez, Mom," I said. "You grilled me every other day when you called."

"I know, honey. But it's different when you're standing right here. You've grown a few inches taller."

To this day, my mother still says this phrase to me even though I stopped growing in the eleventh grade. I think it's because she's shrinking. She must have sensed the tenseness in my neck because she peered over my shoulder.

"Diane's been asking about you."

"What did she say?" I was dying to get over there.

"She's asked at least once a day when you were getting home. She must really like you to write you a letter."

"I guess." I pumped my shoulders, trying to mask my enthusiasm, torn between pumping my mother for information or to ending this close encounter so I could run across the street.

"Do you like her?"

My blood ran cold, her question throwing me into a perplexed state of panic. How should I answer such a question? She meant did I like her as a boyfriend likes a girlfriend, which scared me. I'd always considered Diane to be my girlfriend, and everyone at school knew we were, but to have your mother know kind of gave a kid the willies.

"She's alright, I guess." I don't think my feigned demonstration of indifference was going to win me any Academy Awards.

"That's what I thought. Why don't you go see her? We'll talk about the farm later."

I dropped my backpack and tried to appear casual

as I strolled the driveway toward the street. Diane remained unmoving, watching me. Once to the street, I trotted across the asphalt and into her yard. My mind erupted with a sappy orchestra playing, conjuring images of the two of us running together in slow motion. I managed to expunge the notion when I realized I'd watched one too many corny love movies with my aunt over the summer. There wasn't much else to do at night in the middle of Nowhere Nebraska. I slowed my trot to a quick, but casual pace. Diane took a step toward me, studying my face.

We stood in an awkward silence, far from the reunion either of us expected. I thought I'd be full of talk, but instead my brain turned into a mind-numbing mush, and a solitary phrase couldn't trudge its way through to my conscious thought.

"Hi," I said. *Wow, great opener there, Jack.*

"Hi. You made it home, huh?"

"Yeah, it was a long drive."

"Did you get my letter before you left?"

Heat flushed my cheeks. "Yeah, thanks. It was pretty cool."

She burst into an embarrassed smile and dropped her chin, leaving me a view of her mass of dark curls. When she raised her eyes, a ruddy hue swathed her cheeks, unsure of the next step to take.

"Do you want to go swing in the backyard?" she asked.

"That sounds alright."

She could have asked if I wanted to slice off my hand with a dull, rusty knife, and I would have said yes as long as we could do it together.

We made our way around to the side of the house. Diane pulled open the gate and waited for me to enter before closing it behind us, stopping when the latch clicked shut. Her face was cherry red, burning, as if she'd ran a marathon. At last, she embraced me, squeezing me as hard as my mother. Between the two of them, I would need an x-ray to ensure I didn't crack a couple of ribs. She kissed my lips, just brushing the skin.

"I missed you, Jack," she said before running off toward the swing set. My feet anchored to the grass, unsure of what to do. She'd caught me off guard, and it took my mind a moment to register I'd received my first kiss. My lips tingled in remembrance, marking the sweetest, gentlest kiss in the history of mankind.

"I missed you too, Diane," I whispered, chasing after her to the rusty swings in their tiny backyard, eager to tell her of my summer without her.

CHAPTER SIX

In the summer of 1979, Diane visited the famous Nebraska farm with my parents for a weekend. How she talked her father into letting her go out-of-state with my family, much less go with the sole purpose to meet with yours truly, was nothing short of a miracle. I wouldn't be surprised if Mrs. Riven authorized the trip under the mantra of "it is better to beg for forgiveness than ask for permission".

My aunt spent the entire weekend ogling Diane from across the table. When asked, my mother said it was because she and Uncle Will were childless, and Diane reminded her of the daughter she'd never have.

"Did my parents bug you driving up?" I asked as we snuck outside after dinner, alone for the first time since she pulled into the farmhouse driveway.

"No, they were really nice. They bought me soda and we played the license plate game."

I rolled my eyes at the thought of the asinine license plate venture initiated by my parents on any car ride lasting more than sixty minutes. The endeavor was a futile attempt to find a license plate from each state in the Union. For one thing, it was a diversionary tactic to keep the kids occupied and quiet. It was also the height of inconvenience to play sitting on your knees for five hours because you were too short to see out the window. Plus, my dad was too cheap to buy the scoreboard you could get for fifty cents at any Stuckey's gift shop, so we ended up arguing if we'd already counted the inevitable Texas plate.

As we talked, I led Diane around the barnyard under the cover of rain logged clouds that offered a welcome respite from the blazing early evening sun. She flashed mild interest in the different animals my uncle kept, but was smitten by Hoofer, my aunt's mare. Diane cooed and stroked the horse's nose and giggled when Hoofer ate a carrot out of her hand. I promised her my uncle would take us for a ride tomorrow.

"Where's this fort you wrote me about?"

"Come on, I'll show you." I hopped off the well-worn rail of the horse stall and led the way down the dirt path.

The fort was all mine that summer. Jake decided to spend the months working at a local car wash back home for minimum wage in the vain hope of obtaining a car at the end of the summer for school. My parents wouldn't have allowed it in a million years, even if Jake was able to raise enough cash. They tried to force him to come with them for the weekend, but succumbed to his fervent protests. Dad said he expected to come home to a party-wrecked house, and I asked him if I could have Jake's room after he killed him. My dad told me I was too smart for being eleven.

We made our way along the well-worn path leading to the fort, darting around the outstretched limbs and hopping over massive exposed roots of the nearby trees. Knowing Diane was coming, I hid the old Playboys underneath a nearby rock and covered it with leaves. I'd come back at least a dozen times to make sure they hadn't magically reappeared back on the wood stump coffee table.

During the summer, I trimmed the pathway of weeds and cleared it of any large rocks so I could drag my rusty red wagon here without dumping its contents. I was anxious for Diane to see the fruits of my labor.

"Wow. This is so cool, Jack."

She was as impressed with my work as I was proud of it. Over the course of the summer, I replaced the rotting roof of the clubhouse with a large piece of pinewood my uncle found in his flea market barn. I painted the outside of the fort white with some old paint I'd found in an abandoned corner of the barn. Though there was scarcely enough paint for one coat, it covered the decades old wood rather well. The best part was the carpet my aunt donated to the cause, attributable to her burning desire for new carpeting in the living room. It was a tacky shade of puke green with a mystery rust stain in one corner which looked suspiciously like dried blood, but sufficed as a floor for the tiny shack. Diane took a seat in one of the two rusty chairs I also retrieved from the barn and studied the rippling creek running thirty feet in front of the fort. Though rain failed to kiss our skies for the last three weeks, the runoff from my Uncle's fields kept the water moving at a brisk pace.

"Do you come here a lot?" she asked.

"Sometimes, when I get bored watching the news with Uncle Will and Aunt Kate."

"Even at night?"

"Sure. I used to never come here when it's dark, but now it's pretty cool. You can sit here and watch the fireflies and listen to the frogs. If it gets too dark, I light the lantern my uncle bought for me."

"I'd be scared."

"I do get spooked sometimes, but I just run to the house."

Diane accepted this statement without a word. Most girls would have made fun of you for admitting fear. But, after two years, Diane and I learned to accept the faults of each other without question.

We relaxed in silence for a while, entranced by the rippling creek and being together again. Diane spied the school picture she gave me last year tacked to the side of the fort. It was the one thing on the walls. She stared at it for a moment before turning her eyes to me. Without a word, she reached over and took my hand in hers. I squeezed her hand, echoing her sentiments. I wished the moment would last forever.

CHAPTER SEVEN

When the 1980 school year rolled around, a new family entered the neighborhood. The Washington clan hailed from the great state of Florida, transferred to Kansas City by Mrs. Washington's company. She was an advertising exec who landed a lucrative job with a local firm. It was the subject of scandalous neighborhood scuttlebutt as few husbands followed their wives across the country because of *their* work. Jim and Connie Washington brought with them a rambunctious lad by the name of Michael. When they moved into the house next door to mine, Diane and I watched from her front step with wary eyes as the movers unloaded the van.

"Do you think they have kids?" she asked.

"Probably, check out the bicycle. I'll bet it's a kid's, unless the dad is a midget."

Diane laughed, her face lighting up. I couldn't believe twenty-four months as a couple had flown by. I just returned last week from Uncle Will and Aunt Kate's farm where I experienced my best summer ever. Though I missed Diane, we kept in touch through phone calls and several letters which didn't say much. Neither of us was adept at expressing what we felt and still too young to comprehend it anyway.

An hour later, a large blue station wagon pulled in front of the house across the street. A lanky man with a balding head and elven ears emerged, followed by a pretty, but chunky redhead on the passenger's side. Our new neighbors had arrived.

The second Mike Washington climbed out of the backseat, I knew he would fit right in. He was tan and pudgy in build, with a mass of black hair hanging far too long for the midwest topping his head. He spotted us and we returned his wave. Mike said something to his mother and crossed the street toward us. As he approached, I realized he wasn't so much pudgy as thick. He would later grow into a tall, well-built athlete.

He flashed a mouth full of metal. Diane and I turned ten shades of envy at the braces. Up to a certain age, kids think braces are cool. It isn't until a couple of years later they became unfashionable.

"Hi," I said. "I'm Jack. This is Diane."

"I'm Mike. We moved here from Florida."

"What grade are you in, Mike?" Diane asked.

"Sixth. It sucks. I was finally going to be the oldest in the school when my mom's job made us move."

I nodded in empathy. That would suck. "We're in sixth grade too. Maybe you'll be in our class."

We hung around talking about nothing, much the way sixth graders do. We conversed on the utter coolness of The Empire Strikes Back and debated if Darth Vader was really Luke's father. When Diane yawned in boredom, we switched to the topic of neighborhood do's and don'ts. It was imperative Mike avoid being seen with any of the geeks. It would be a devastating blow for the new kid in the school. Without sounding conceited, we told him he could hang out with us on his first day. I'd watched

Diane during the entire interlude, judging her reaction to Mike, remembering the Gill Summers affair last year.

Gill Summers, a freckled, crewcut carrot-topped kid, moved to the area in the middle of school last year. I struck up a conversation with him at recess and thought he was pretty cool. I invited him to my house after school to hang out, but Diane told me it was a mistake. Something about Gill rubbed her wrong.

We lounged in my family room watching Bosom Buddies—nothing quite like Tom Hanks in drag for humor. Diane declined my invitation to join us, which was odd because there were few people in our little world Diane didn't like. I kept checking out Gill, but couldn't spot the negative she glimpsed in him. It became obvious as the evening wore on as he peeled back his obnoxious layers like an onion until we got to the rotted bulb at the core.

Gill laughed too loud, didn't close the door to the bathroom or flush the toilet, talked throughout the show, pointing out what was on the screen like we were all blind and couldn't see it for ourselves, and jumped up during an ad for Soul Train and danced the weirdest little jig like he auditioned for a spot on the show. Even my mother's eyebrows shot off the top of her head in question.

Gill was barely out the door when my dad turned to me. "What in the hell is wrong with that kid? If you ever act that stupid, I'll disown you."

It took three weeks to convince Gill to leave me alone-my reputation at school damaged but salvageable.

I learned my lesson and listened to Diane's uncanny ability to judge people. It was as if they emitted an aura only she envisioned. She must have liked the aura around Mike

Washington, because she echoed my sentiments about his hanging out with us at school. If she didn't like him, she would give me "the look" and I wouldn't issue the invitation. It was an unspoken sign we'd often use in the years ahead.

Mike said his goodbyes and crossed the street to silence his mother who called him to help unpack. Diane and I soon parted as she was going back-to-school shopping with her mother. My mother and I already weathered the blood-thirsty crowds at K-Mart a few days ago in the cut-throat search for the right Trapper Keeper notebook. I crossed the street and took one last glance back at Diane who was doing the same, her hand on her front door, waiting for me to turn around as I always did. I was the luckiest guy in the world.

CHAPTER EIGHT

To be in sixth grade and at the top of the social heap was an exhilarating experience. You towered over the other kids, you did real school work as the teachers prepared you for the rigors of junior high and life was good. We knew enough to savor the moment, knowing we would plummet to the bottom of the totem pole again next year.

In sixth grade, you chose your lunch table in the cafeteria and commanded the playground, getting the best choice of kickballs, gloves and bats. The younger kids trembled with fear when you stepped to the dodge ball wall with your arsenal in check. Best of all, in sixth grade you knew it was your last year in that damn building—the last of Mr. Johnson's torture in gym class, the last of Ms. Byron's tyranny in the library and the last of Estelle, the cafeteria cook, her inedible creations and the meteor mole with the hair coming out.

In Social Studies, we covered real current events like John Lennon's assassination, some guy named Saddam launching a war in Iran over oil and the impact of the United States hockey team beating Russia. Mrs. France found a way of bringing real issues to our level. We felt more adult than at any other time in our young academic lives.

Whoever devised the educational system where you go
to separate establishments for grade school, junior high and high
school was a genius. Nothing could better prepare you for life
than going through those ups and downs, reveling at your time on
the top before crawling your way from the bottom. The hierarchy
experience matched any job I've ever taken.

During the first couple of months of the school year,
Mike, Diane and I grew into quite the trio. Mike hung out with us
most of the time when we played outside at recess or in Diane's
backyard, which made Diane kind of jealous at first. However,
Mike seemed to know when she and I wanted to hang out
together and would go find something to do. But, for the most
part, we found out the three of us enjoyed the same interests and
liked being around each other. In a matter of weeks, Mike moved
from the status of unknown new neighbor to my best male
friend.

We had a blast in school though we landed in Mrs.
Tucker's narrow-eyed crosshairs for talking too much in class.
We traded football pencils you could get out of the classroom
dispenser for a dime, passed notes back and forth in class making
fun of Gill Summers and ruled the gym class flag football team.
We were kings of the hill to be certain.

While Mike and I had fun, Diane seemed content hanging
in the background, watching us make asses out of ourselves,
which we did as often as possible. Once in a blue moon, she
participated in our mischievous acts of juvenilism.

At home, Jake took the forefront of most conversations
over the trouble he kept finding himself in, despite the fact that,
at least according to Jake, nothing was ever his fault. I think if he
would ever own up to any of his blunders instead of concocting

some convoluted story, my father would have gone a lot easier on him. My father, though, was bound by paternal law to play the game of "I know you're lying and I know you know that I know you're lying, but I can't prove it."

I must admit, it was nice having a delinquent older brother. Jake getting busted for skipping school, or for drinking beer at a party and puking in the car, made my outbursts and spitwads at school trivial in the grand scheme of things. He even tried to blame some of his juvenile acts on his depression over the drinking binge death of Led Zepplin's drummer, John Bonham. Of course, my father cut him zero slack. Jake was a huge Zepplin fan, but even that excuse stretched the bounds of lameness.

Mom played the housewife, though I could tell she was getting restless. She worried about getting old and useless, though nary a line was visible on her pretty face. I overheard her talking to my dad as he read the paper in our breakfast nook while mom cooked dinner. Dad said they were fine and didn't need the extra money. Mom replied she was so bored during the day she thought about having an affair with the milkman or running off with J.R. Ewing from the show Dallas. I wasn't entirely sure what an affair entailed and knew we didn't have a milkman so her reference eluded me. Though she meant it as a joke, I don't think Dad found it humorous.

In the heart of holiday shopping, my mother took a part-time job at a retail clothing store. She worked during the day, with an occasional night shift thrown in, but she was usually home by the time I arrived. Jake and I loved it when she worked nights because Dad would raid the cupboards for a few fruitless minutes before announcing we were going out to dinner or ordering pizza. I couldn't figure out why he went through this futile search the cupboard exercise because Dad would burn the water if he tried to boil it. The one meal he'd tried to prepare set off every smoke alarm in the house and would have sent his offspring to the emergency room if it hadn't been for our liberal consumption of the chalky, pink elixir Pepto-Bismol.

With Christmas approaching, I found myself in a quandary as to what I should get Diane for her present. Gifts for the family was easy thanks to an empty wallet and zero expectations that I have any money. Mom bought Dad's present from me, and Dad did the same for Mom. For Mike, I wrapped one of my comic books to complete his Iron Man collection. But Diane should get something special, something from the heart. If I wrapped something I already owned and gave it to her, she would respond with a punch in my gut. Even with Mom's new job, I couldn't ask her for help getting a present for my girlfriend. So, I made the biggest mistake in my young life—I asked my brother Jake for help.

Jake rocked in his room, headphones on and the music cranked to such a volume that Rush's *Working Man* blared clear as day. It's no wonder the man can't hear anything to this day unless you scream into his ear canal. Watching a war movie at his house is like being thrown into the battle yourself, the furniture vibrating with each monstrous explosion.

My dad tried bribing him to cut the scraggly brown hair draping over his brow, obscuring his beady little eyes. "I'm going to get you a dress for Christmas, son. Maybe you'll get lucky and some guy will ask you to prom."

If the jab affected Jake, he didn't show it. He thumbed

through a magazine of cars he couldn't afford while picking at the acne which exploded over his face like a scarred battlefield. At sixteen, his gaunt appearance and sunken eyes were eerily similar to a strung-out heroin addict, though to my knowledge he hadn't touched anything harder than liquor. At least, that's the data my invasive reconnaissance missions into his room yielded.

He noticed me at the doorway and squinted those pea eyes in disbelief, as if he couldn't comprehend I sullied the gate of his castle, begging for admittance into the kingdom.

"What the hell do you want, buttface?" the King asked, not bothering to take off the headphones.

"I want to ask you something," I said.

"What?" he shouted, getting the clue to take off the headset.

"I said I want to ask you something," I said, shouting to combat the music blasting into his ears.

"Jesus, you don't have to yell, you moron." He waited with his mop head, pizza stained t-shirt, ratty bell-bottom jeans, and dirty uncovered feet. I realized I may have made a mistake coming here. What would this guy know about love?

"Well? What the hell do you want? I ain't got all day."

I rubbed my nervous hands together. "It's almost Christmas, Jake." It was an unending walk on eggshells with Jake. The wrong words would send him into a brotherly frenzy, ending with my head shoved in the toilet.

"So?"

"Well, I can't figure out what to get for Diane."

"Who the hell is Diane?" Jake liked to say the word hell. It was the closest thing he could say in the way of a curse word without getting yelled at by my parents. If he even whispered a stronger obscenity, my mother's radar would ping and she'd make a beeline to Jake's bedroom. I'd witnessed it before and it wasn't pretty.

"You know…my girlfriend…Diane."

It took him a minute to register who I talked about, forcing me to wonder if he messed with me or if he was just plain stupid. I decided to go with the latter.

Jake arched his eyebrows. "Your girlfriend, eh? Did you score with her yet?"

"No." I crossed my arms, unsure what he meant by "score." Mike and I debated over the technical definition of a "score" using the old baseball analogy and decided you had to reach second base before a "score" could be tallied up. Our evolution to the homerun mentality remained a few years away.

Jake threw his hands up. "Just askin', twerp. Geez, don't get so defensive. It makes a difference on what you have to get her."

"Well, I did kiss her a couple of times," I offered.

"Tongue?" He scooted to the edge of the bed, stroking his chin and soaking in my reply as if he were the great Hercule Poirot on the trail of a devious, murdering scoundrel.

Tongue? You could do that? "No way, Jake."

"Good," he said, rocking his head. "You can get off cheap."

Oh, brother, I thought. Though sharing the depths of my love life with Jake would yield little or nothing, I was curious about the ideas his hamster brain would generate.

"How much money do you have?"

"Six bucks," I said with a sigh. It wasn't much. A crisp twenty-dollar bill graced my pocket earlier in the month before

Mike and I discovered a new comic book store within biking distance. Now I had a pile of Spider-Man's and an empty wallet. In retrospect, I should have planned my finances a little better, a feat I didn't manage until well into my adult years.

"Six bucks, eh? Well, little brother, with my employee discount at Bargain Barn, I could probably snag you something pretty cool."

"Like what?" I was skeptical of his offer and for good reason. A few months ago, I gave him three dollars for a game and came away with nothing but a bruised arm when he punched me for telling Dad he stole my money. Dad slipped three bucks back in my palm, but nothing came from Jake including an apology.

"Man, I don't know. I'd have to look. Just give me the money, and I'll pick something up for you tonight."

"I don't know, Jake. Last time you took my money and I didn't get anything."

Jake scowled, sweeping the hair out of his eyes, and started to rise off the bed. I took a step back, worried he would rush me, but he settled back and his eyes spit fire in my direction.

"Man, that was a long time ago and you got it back anyway."

"From Dad."

Jake scooted back to the headboard of the bed as he picked up the still blaring headphones. "Hey, if you don't want my help then piss off."

"No, wait. I'm sorry," I said. For some unknown reason, I wanted his help. I wanted the wisdom someone his age could bring. I'd observed Jake with girls before, so he must have some rudimentary knowledge of the female sex. One time, my mom and I went to the Bargain Barn to pick him up and found him making out with a razor-thin blonde my mom called "a little tramp." I couldn't detect her level of trampiness, but some measure of pride rippled at my older brother with a girl. He'd talked about it for so long, it was nice to know he wasn't completely full of shit.

Jake represented a textbook definition of a "wannabe." For all his bravado, I think he was a scared kid trying to fit in wherever he could. He wielded as much athletic talent as my grandmother in her wheelchair at the nursing home, so he was out with the jocks. If you looked up slob in the dictionary, there'd be a picture of Jake with his wrinkled, baggy clothes with more stains and holes than a tattered kitchen rag at a pizza joint. He wasn't smart enough for the academic clubs and thought Thespians involved girl on girl sex acts. No, the groups willing to take Jake in their fold were the other societal castaways and miscreants. It presented a slippery slope to be sure and, as much torture as my big brother inflicted on me, I hoped he would maintain solid footing and avoid the plummet to the gully of losers at its base.

"Look, tomorrow's Christmas Eve, dude. You're running out of time. You come up snake eyes on the gift and it'll be a long, cold winter."

I reached my hand into my pocket, fingering the meager wad of six folded bills against my palm. The precarious scales of trust swayed in my mind. Trust Jake or ask Mom. Jake might come through and get something cool. My mom would definitely get something corny and embarrass me. She might even make me go with her, and I would rather slide naked down a slide of broken glass and land in a pool of rubbing alcohol before I'd go shopping with my mom.

I pulled the thin pack of bills, my brain screaming at the stupidity of my idea. Seeing no other recourse, I caved and handed the last of my money to him. He cackled, counting the bills off one at a time, as if it was a wad of Ben Franklin's instead of George Washington's.

"You won't be sorry, little brother. You won't be sorry."

Despite his reassuring words, the lead ball settling in the pit of my twelve-year-old stomach told me I would, indeed, be very sorry.

CHAPTER NINE

On Christmas morning, shards of plastic packaging
and festive paper littered our living room floor like a wrapping
paper factory exploded and spewed its debris on our orange
shag carpet. My mother scrambled to save the colorful bows
for next year while Jake and I moved from box to box as if we
were Olympians vying for the gold medal for present opening.
My dad sunk in his weathered brown recliner, sipping a cup of
coffee and glowering in disbelief at the number of pairs of socks
and underwear he received from his loving family. He'd spent
hundreds of dollars on us, fulfilling each reasonable whim and
desire, and received in return what my mother thought he needed
most, but wanted least.

When the dust from the present opening carnage settled,
it was a bountiful Christmas in the Phipps's household, and I
could tell Dad landed the bonus he worried about. Most of
the things I circled in the toy section of the Sears catalog lay
arranged in front of me. I scored the G.I. Joe with the Kung Fu
grip, the Six Million Dollar Man action figure with the bionic eye
you could peer through, my Evel Knieval stunt bike and a brand
spanking new three speed bicycle which my mom somehow
managed to wrap. My grandmother wrapped up the obligatory

sweaters and other clothes, but at twelve you don't count those in the loot you scored. It was traditional fare.

Jake scored a new record player and some rock-n-roll albums he wanted, though I was quite surprised my parents purchased them. The way my dad yelled at him to "turn that crap down," I would have expected him to get Jake a Waylon Jennings or Willie Nelson album, music more suited to my father's tastes. He also received the standard clothes presents from Grandma Helen, though he hated them and proclaimed he'd burn them.

G.I. Joe and Steve Austin battled to the death on the edge of the coffee table when the doorbell rang.

"Diane, sweetie," my mother crooned from the entryway. In an instant, my blood chilled to ice water. The present. Oh, crap. I had no clue as to the location or contents of Jake's Bargain Barn purchase. I forgot to ask and was utterly screwed.

"Come in. Jack's in the living room."

"Thanks, Mrs. Phipps," Diane said. She entered the living room, gorgeous in a stylish Christmas plaid dress and a long red overcoat, her long dark curls hanging to the middle of the lapels. But, the package in her hand with my name on it froze the ice water in my blood.

"Merry Christmas, Jack," she said, holding a box out to me with a flash of her pearly whites. I surmised from the wrapping job she'd done it herself. It didn't have the professional look only a mother could achieve. I think they sent moms to present wrapping school at some point, perhaps a section of their Lamaze classes. My mother was a master at the art of wrapping. She could wrap a Boeing 747 with a single roll of paper and three pieces of Scotch tape and leave no spot exposed. I took the present from Diane.

"Merry Christmas. How was it at your house?" I stalled and hoped she couldn't tell.

"Good. I got lots of neat stuff." She searched the room for a box with her name on it.

"Me too. Want to play with some of my presents?"

"Maybe later." She eyeballed the package in my hand. "Open your present first."

I stared at the package, afraid of what it might hold considering the fact I didn't know if I'd officially gotten her anything. Jake slipped in late last night, and in the excitement of opening my presents, I forgot to find out what he purchased for Diane with my hard-earned cash, if he got anything at all. I opened Diane's package slower than I'd opened anything in my entire life, excuses for my failure to get her anything flailing like a drowning victim as they attempted to surface on my train of conscious. I peeled back the paper with a care reserved for the handling of the original Declaration of Independence, Diane nestling close on the couch.

When I couldn't stall any longer and was forced to open the box, her icy blue eyes locked on my face, waiting for my reaction. I peeled back the lid to the box, speechless at what lay inside.

It was a framed photo of Diane and I sitting on her front steps last summer, the moment forever captured in black and white. I leaned forward in the photo, grinning with my elbows on my knees. Diane rested her head on my shoulder, the corners of her thin lips curled upward. It was by far the best picture we would ever take together. In it, we smiled with the warmth of years together and happy memories, like an old married couple stuck in twelve-year-old bodies. The photo still rests on my dresser to this day.

"Do you like it?" She could tell I did, but wanted to hear it. The image shimmered before me.

"Diane, it's great."

"Really?"

"Really."

"You're not just saying it because I'm sitting here are you?"

"No," I said.

"Are you sure?"

Years later, this badgering would be a source of frustration for me. Diane never seemed to believe any of my compliments, probing for some word to satisfy her desire to please me. I even went to the library at school and poured over a thesaurus finding synonyms for the word "great," but failed to find the magic words, instead relying on my constant assurances I loved whatever she gave me.

"No, if I didn't like it, I would tell you. I like it a lot."

"Good. My mom picked out the frame, but it was my idea for the picture."

"It's perfect. Just perfect."

"Well?" she asked. "Did you get me anything?"

Here was the moment of truth. I couldn't tell her I think I got her something but didn't know what it was. I should have told her the truth, something we'd done in the past and I couldn't fathom why I hesitated at this point. Instead of spilling the beans, I stalled.

I told Diane I left her present in my room. I leapt the stairs two at a time, panic gripping my heart with sharp, steel talons. Jake listened to his new Molly Hatchet album in his room while flipping through the album insert. When he spotted the panic etched on my face, the corners of his mouth slithered up and he took off the headphones.

"Forget something, squirt? I noticed you had company downstairs."

I slapped my hands on my knees, breathing heavy. "Where's her present?"

The two-toned clang of the doorbell rang.

Jake rolled his eyes. "Well, thank you, thank you, older brother. I really appreciate your efforts in scoring a cool gift for my girlfriend. You're the best, you're king."

"Whatever, Jake. Where's the gift?"

"Jack," my mother yelled from downstairs. "Mike's here."

"I'll be right there, Mom," I yelled back. "Come on, man. Where is it?"

"You have to say please," Jake said, hands locked behind his head, enjoying himself. In the meantime, the doorbell sounded again.

"Please, Jake. Where's Diane's present?"

"Jack," my mother yelled again. "Mr. and Mrs. Riven are here too. Come down now."

"Give me a second, Mom." I turned my attention back to my brother who started to piss me off.

"Alright, alright. Don't get your panties in a bunch, little bro." He pressed to his feet and waved his hand toward the door. "Got the box in the car. Let's go get it. You're going to love it."

"What is it?" I asked as we trotted down the stairs.

"Trust me, she'll love it."

Jake mumbled hello to the Rivens before ducking out

46

to the garage where he parked his mongrel car. My father and Jake spent some quality time working on it yesterday before Jake went to work. Dad even let him park it in the garage overnight. I think he would rather have oil stains on the garage floor instead of the driveway. Instead of getting to follow him out to the car, I remained trapped in the living room with Diane, both sets of parents and my buddy Mike who focused on making G.I. Joe execute karate moves. My mom rambled about the picture of Diane and I, begging Mrs. Riven for a copy of the photo, when Jake reentered the room, slipping me a rectangular box wrapped in cheesy red reindeer paper. He leaned over and whispered in my ear.

"You owe me a quarter for the wrap job."

Relief swept through me as nobody witnessed Jake slip me the box. I would wait until the crowd left, and Diane and I were alone which would provide me with the opportunity to explain the gift in the event Jake got something stupid. To be honest, I was pretty happy he didn't spend my six bucks on himself. For now, I planned to lay low and set the present on the coffee table, hidden behind the wooden carving of Jesus in the manger.

"Diane gave you this great picture, Jack," my mother said. "What did you get her?"

The capillaries in my face dilated, flushing my skin in crimson. "I haven't given it to her yet. It's upstairs."

"No, Jack. It's right here," Jake said, slithering close and grabbing the box.

I glared into the yellow-toothed evil smirk of my arch nemesis. My fears were well-founded as I knew whatever Jake scored for me at Bargain Barn wasn't good. His leer scared me the most, like the devil himself on the verge of snatching a soul from the hands of God. He would enjoy this and his joy spelled pain for me.

"Give it to her, Jack," my mom said.

My face flushed red. "Mom, not in front of everybody."

"Why not?" Mr. Riven's nostrils flared. If I didn't give his daughter the present now, God only knew what he'd think I planned to give her. On the other hand, if I gave it to her and it sucked, I would be hosed anyway. Jake's hot, peanut butter breath heated the back of my neck, and I clutched the box to keep from backhanding him. He'd planned this and wouldn't let the chance to nail me in front of everyone pass him by.

The crowd in the room ogled me. Even Mike, who knew the details of the whole sordid affair, couldn't bail me out. I sighed and handed the box to my girlfriend. Diane smiled and accepted the gift, shaking the box. My clenched fists carved half-moon shapes into my palms as she tore off the paper. The crowd drew in closer as if the final resting place of the Lost Ark of the Covenant lay in the bottom of the box. I was as curious as they were because I knew as little about the gift as they did. Only my stupid brother was privy to its contents.

I closed my eyes before she took off the box lid and waited for the reactions. I just needed a couple of oohs and aahs. Come on, ooh. Come on, ahhh. Lady Luck, paint me a pathway to the Promised Land. I prayed for the absence of hysterical screams from my mother or a thud of Mrs. Riven's fainted frame on our hardwood floor. But, when I opened the box, I think my mother and Mrs. Riven were too shocked to say anything.

"What in the hell is that?" Mr. Riven said, breaking the unbearable silence.

I let my eyes creep open, knowing their reactions spelled doom for me. Jake laughed so hard he couldn't catch his breath and thumped to the floor, rolling in hysterics. Diane, my girlfriend for as long as I could remember, the love of my young life held up my Christmas offering to her. My mouth dropped in horror and embarrassment, and my once icy blood boiled.

"Just what in God's name is wrong with your boy, Phipps?" Mr. Riven curled his lips back in a snarl. "What kind of present is that for a twelve-year-old girl?"

"Oh, Jack, what were you thinking?" my mother asked, before running from the room in embarrassment.

I could offer nothing in my defense for I was as shocked and angry as I think I ever would be. My life was over thanks to a buck-toothed, greasy haired punk for a brother who now took great joy in my misery and suffering. I leapt over the couch and pummeled him with my fists. While the adults quarreled and Mike attempted to pull me off Jake, Diane remained quiet. She sat on the floral couch, amid the madness and hysteria, and stared in wide-eyed disbelief at the pink training bra she held in her hands.

CHAPTER NINE

We received the call on a blistering day in the summer of 1982 as I played whiffle ball in my backyard with Mike and Diane, and a group of other neighborhood kids. We lined out the bases—the flower pot by the steps, the base of Mom's ash tree that refused to grow but she wouldn't get rid of, the cement slab where a rusted basketball goal used to sit and the corner of the garage for home plate. A twelve-foot-high hedge we named the Green Monster ran along the backside of our property.

Ronny Tobin, an obnoxious, red-headed goofball, who hit like Babe Ruth, brought over his mammoth, flat plastic bat which we used to bash apart little plastic whiffle balls. I sent one after another soaring over the Green Monster before trotting in triumph around the bases. Ronny protested after my sixth homerun in seven at bats and tried to make some absurd rule limiting the number of homeruns one person could hit. When I called him on it, he declared since he owned the bat, only his team could wield it. While this strategy proved effective with my other teammates, I was the Wiffleball Master and answered his challenge with my own bat by blasting an opposite field seventh homerun over the fence.

My annual journey to the farm in Nebraska was hours

away. My dad ran to a jobsite to finish a few things, but we would depart as soon as he got back. I had my suitcase and a box full of entertainment necessities stashed by the front door, ready to be loaded into the family station wagon. I'd miss Mike and the other guys from the neighborhood as it's impossible to get a good game of anything going in the far reaches of the Nebraska farmlands. But, more than anything, I'd miss Diane and the grand opportunity to see her face each day.

Diane began the inevitable change from child to young woman after the beginning of the new year. Her china doll face elongated, giving her a hint of the cover girl looks she would one day possess. Her tight black curls relaxed, and she began to experiment with make-up and lipstick when her parents weren't home. But, the most dramatic feature change was her bosom.

The training bra I "gave" her for Christmas turned out to be a necessary device anyway, a fact mattering little to the interested parties in observance that day. The meaning of the line in Bob Seger's song *Night Moves* clicked into place for me—"Points all her own sitting way up high." I became fixated on them, watching when she wasn't looking, hoping they'd grow before my eyes. Ever since I'd found the old man's Playboy collection in the back of his closet, I prayed Diane would develop a healthy chest. It's terrible, I know, but the thought of it was mighty exciting.

Jake's bra prank upset Diane every bit as much as it pissed me off. Once explained, she forgave me, though the ember of anger still burned in her eyes. At least she directed the ember in the vicinity of my brother. My parents went ballistic when I explained what happened. In the past, they sent me from the room when they chewed Jake out, but they were so mad at him they forgot about little old me in the corner, watching the carnage with tremendous pleasure. My dad used curse words in the one-way tirade I hadn't even heard before, and I wondered if he made some of them up.

Following my final homerun trot, my dad pulled into the driveway and directed the neighborhood kids to head to their respective homes. Mike and I said goodbye, giving each other high fives. Diane stayed without protest from my father.

I followed Dad through the basement and up the stairs to the living room, the long-awaited nuptials of Prince Charles and Diana Spencer playing on the television. My mother perched on the couch with the telephone receiver pressed to her ear. From her trembling jaw and haunted eyes, it wasn't good news from the other end.

"Honey," my father said, noting the tears shimmering in her eyes. "What is it?"

"Okay," my mother said into the receiver with a choked voice. "We'll be there as soon as we can."

My heart stopped as I lingered in the doorway. The one other time I saw her with that expression was when she'd gotten the news Grandma Moonie passed away. She sat in the exact same spot on the couch, held the phone receiver in exact manner and cast the same look of complete and utter heartbreak to my father. My father dropped to her side on the couch, taking her hand as she hung up the phone.

"Oh God, Barbara," my father whispered. "What happened?"

After struggling for a moment to compose herself, she reached a trembling hand to his face, resting it on his cheek.

"Will was killed this morning."

My mind went numb, her words echoing in my head. Will was killed this morning. Images of my Uncle Will raced through my mind, and hot, salty tears surged to my eyes. They rolled across my cheek as Diane's arm slipped around my shoulders.

"What?" A blank and empty disbelief clouded my father's features. "How?"

My mother's voice hitched as tears slid down her face. "Kate said there was an accident with the auger in a grain bin. The auger caught his leg and pulled him in. Oh, honey, I'm so sorry."

My father's jaw and his lanky frame trembled before he broke, sobbing on my mother's chest. My father was the strongest man I'd ever known or would ever know. He'd weathered Grandma's funeral without the slightest hint of a tear, though the sorrow swam across his features. I thought nothing could shake his foundation. Now, to watch my pillar, my idol weeping in anguish over the loss of his brother was more than I could bear. The tears flowed, carving salty trails on my dirty cheeks. Diane's arm slipped from my shoulders as I walked to my parents who clutched each other, my mother stroking my dad's head.

I couldn't fathom the fact Uncle Will was dead. I reached out to my father and though I couldn't comprehend his agony, I wanted him to stop crying. The mere sight of it tore my soul apart. My father reached his arm around and pulled me to him. My mother's arm joined his around my back and the three of us huddled there mourning. It was one of the worst moments of my life.

We made the journey to Nebraska for the funeral in silence with the exception of a talk radio show's discussion of the fifty-two hostages being held in Iran. Pretty boring stuff, but I didn't want to ask my dad to change it. A couple of times my dad tried to make small talk, but when you responded to his inquiries, he would gaze ahead at the highway and you knew he didn't hear a word you said. My mother watched the scenery flash by in silence as we rolled up I-29, an ever-present wad of tissue in her hand. She took Uncle Will's death as hard as my father. I think he was the brother she never had.

Jake and I made a deal with each other before we left that we wouldn't aggravate our parents on the drive. During past trips, one of us would eventually take up too much room in the backseat, resulting in the inevitable invisible line being drawn across the center of the seat dividing our respective territories. Jake would torture me by touching my side. I would yell at him, Mom would yell at both of us and my father would issue his empty threat of turning the car around and heading home. Jake and I both knew there was zero chance he'd follow through with the threat two hundred miles from home, but it shut us up anyway. During this trip, however, we both figured Mom and Dad had enough to deal with and kept our mouths shut.

"Anybody hungry?" my dad asked. "There's a McDonald's at the next exit."

My stomach growled. "I could eat."

"Me too," Jake said.

My mom and dad locked eyes, but said nothing. He reached out and took her hand, and minutes later we drove past the exit. Jake and I watched the golden arches fade away into the distance. We glanced at each other and shrugged.

"I hope Kate's holding up," my mom said.

"She'll be alright," my father said. "She's a strong

woman."

"But they've been together almost as long as we have. I couldn't imagine what I'd do without you."

With those words, my dad released her hand and wiped his eyes. He held together well after his initial cry on the couch. He pressed to his feet, told us to pack some clothes, including our suits and headed into the bedroom. Sixty minutes later we were on the road. I told Diane I'd call her later, and she responded with a quick hug and a kiss on the cheek. She waved to me from the window of her house when we pulled out of the driveway.

Uncle Will was my father's older brother, three years his senior. They grew up together in the same farmhouse my aunt and uncle lived in. I used to love watching Dad and Uncle Will get together, drink a few beers and tell childhood stories. A champion storyteller, my Uncle Will could weave a yarn about their teenage years with such amazing detail you heard the sound of things, saw the colors and styles of people's clothing, and felt the weather that particular day to the temperature. It was like watching a movie. A story of a ten-minute occurrence would take an hour to lay out, an additional thirty minutes added if they'd drank more than a six-pack. Those stories were magical, no matter how many times he told them.

My dad said he should get a tape recorder and lock in some of these stories. From those, he could write a book about their years in the country and make a million dollars. Years after Uncle Will's death, Dad took paper to pen and tried to write the saga. Though he did it well, it just wasn't the same.

Hours later, we pulled off the asphalt highway onto a gravel road. We bounced across the washboards in the road and fishtailed on the buildup of gravel at the road's edges. These tricky roads might have made some people nervous, but I held complete faith in my father. He and Uncle Will cruised these roads thousands of times before.

My already dour mood dipped further south as we closed in on the farm. The brisk wind of the plains moaned across the knee-high corn stalks my uncle planted, and I wondered who would harvest them. I recalled the summer before last when I didn't want to come here at all because of Diane. I'd ridden in a pouty silence, refusing to even peek out the window at the vistas that once spelled summer fun. This time, however, I took it in as if it would be my last trip. I studied the detail of the cows at the local feedlot and noted the irony of the name of the road running alongside of it—Sweet Water Avenue. I soaked in the one room schoolhouse my father, Uncle Will and Aunt Kate attended. My dad commented in jealousy at the jungle gym equipment rusting in the front yard followed by a nauseating rendition of "we didn't have any of that when we were kids." If you believed my father, he played with nothing but dirt and sticks growing up and was thankful to have them. I drank it all in as we neared the farmhouse, savoring the scene as one would a fine meal.

A dozen dusty pickups congregated in the driveway leading to my aunt and uncle's house. As we climbed out, the lush fields of corn whispered in the hot Nebraska sun, Uncle Will's land he wouldn't harvest again. The mere sight of the corn, the barn, even the pig's clanging their feeder lids brought tears to my eyes. As we approached the house, one of Uncle Will's best friends, Randy Taylor, came out and greeted my father with a shake of the hand. The two talked while the rest of us hung around the station wagon. After a minute, they parted ways and we entered the house.

Several people gathered at the dining room table while women I recognized, but couldn't place a name to, scrambled around making coffee and putting cold cuts on a platter. I followed Dad into the living room where Aunt Kate slumped, eyes cast in the direction of the television but failing to register whatever flashed across the screen. Her eyes were bloodshot, her nose red and her hair was a mass of frizzy black and gray. In her lap she held a tissue box, gripping its edges to the point she'd crushed them. The floodgate's opened when she noticed my father, bawling as she rose from her chair to hug him.

"Johnny," she said, clinging to my father. "Oh God, Johnny. What am I going to do?"

"We'll get through it, Katie." My father stroked her hair as Aunt Kate sobbed, rubbing her nose with a balled-up wad of Kleenex.

After a few minutes, Aunt Kate appeared to settle, smoothing the non-existent wrinkles from her clothes. She gave my mother and Jake hugs, accepting their condolences. My feet anchored to the floor, watching them, afraid if I approached I might upset her even more since I would have arrived today anyway, but under different circumstances. She noticed me, put her hands on her hips and threw me a half-hearted smile.

"Aren't you going to give your Aunt Kate a hug, Jack?"

I ran over and threw my arms around her and bawled. Through the tears, I tried to tell her how sorry I was about Uncle Will, how I loved him and how I would stay to help her out on the farm through the summer. I'm sure she couldn't understand a word of it, but she continued to kneel beside me and hold me. While I intended to comfort her, I think she provided me with the comfort and the security. My dad was right; she was a strong woman.

The funeral was a miserable, gut-wrenching experience. My dad gave a heartfelt and humorous eulogy, throwing in a couple of the experiences he and Uncle Will shared. Friends and neighbors also told their favorite memories of Uncle Will. Some of them were funny stories, lifting the spirits of those in attendance at the packed funeral home. Other stories of Uncle Will's tremendous generosity made us sadder for his passing.

It was nice observing how many lives my uncle touched. My father said your legacy isn't what you leave behind, but how those you leave behind remember you. There was nothing like witnessing a theory proven to be true.

As one of the pallbearers, I followed my father from the funeral home, holding the casket with all my might. When we managed to get it into the hearse, my hands ached from the tight grip I'd maintained on the casket handle. My father gave me a tight-lipped pat on the back as we climbed in our car to head to the cemetery.

The deep gravesite made me shudder at the thought of dying and being lowered into the ground. My young mind flashed images of being trapped in the coffin and trying to get out. The minister's words offered little comfort as he read from the Bible, because I didn't understand half of the things he said and instead focused on the coffin with my favorite uncle inside. I wasn't much of a spiritual person, but I liked to imagine he was in heaven. When they lowered him into the ground, I whispered my goodbye and an incredible sadness settled upon my heart. But, I didn't cry. I don't think I had any tears left.

Dad and I toiled side by side with local farmers over the next few days in my uncle's cornfields and around the property. Somehow, he managed to get the time off work. Mom and Jake stayed for several days before heading back to Kansas City. My father tried to get me to go with them.

"Come on, Jack. Go on home," my father said.

"I can't, Dad. I want to stay here and help you."

"We've got plenty of help from the neighbors. Everyone's pitching in." He squatted in front of me and rustled my hair. "We can handle it, sport."

I tried to conjure the words to impart the importance that I stay and help. Jake was dying to get back home, but I would sooner have plucked out my eyebrows with wet, slippery tweezers than to get in our car. Something anchored me here, some business I felt compelled to finish even though I wasn't sure what it was.

"I have to stay. I have to stay and help," I said.

"But why, son?"

"I don't know. Maybe because it's what I was supposed to do anyway this summer. Maybe it's because I think Aunt Kate needs me here, even though there's so many other people around. Something's telling me I can't go home. Not now. I want to be here, here on this farm doing the things Uncle Will taught me how to do."

My father pulled me close and kissed me on the neck. He released me, held me out at arm's length and his teeth shined bright under his grey-flecked stubbled cheeks. "You're a hell of a kid, Jack. I'm awfully proud of you. Unload your bags from the back of the wagon and change your clothes. We've got work to do."

I threw my arms around him before running to the car and grabbing my bag, telling my mom I would stay. She kissed me on the cheek and told me to call her. I asked her to tell Diane I would call soon and tell her what was going on. Sprinting to my room, I threw on my ratty work jeans and a t-shirt from my baseball team before joining my father back outside.

It was the strangest sensation. I was happy, yet still mourning the loss of my uncle and sad at all the stuff we'd never do together. My heart ached at the fact I wouldn't see his toothful grin again, or laugh until I couldn't breathe at his jokes and stories, or ever work side by side with him in the fields.

I realized the reason behind my duty to stay at the farm working with my father. It would provide me with closure. The memory of my uncle would be served by performing the tasks he taught me to do. I would do them and think of him. It was the one thing I could do that would have made Uncle Will happy. Even though it was an uncool thing to do as a twelve-year-old, I reached out and took my father by the hand. Together, we strolled the packed dirt path to the barn just as my uncle and I had countless times over the years. At that moment, I felt closer to both my father and Uncle Will than I ever would again.

CHAPTER TEN

The first day of junior high slapped away my lofty conceptions of middle school. I entered the educational middle ground with great aspirations and hope, but was soon thrown into the realm of obscurity and torment reserved for the low man on the seventh-grade totem pole. I underwent the same torment and mental distress I imagined prisoners of war suffered during their captivity. The only things missing were the bamboo sticks under the fingernails, though the older kids discussed it at length during a session when they crammed me into the skinny hall locker.

My principle tormenter was a mountain of a boy by the name of Renny Hanks—a buzz-cut, white-trash-piece-of-malevolence who ruled the school with an iron fist. He was already six feet tall and weighed two hundred and fifty pounds, a better than average size for a boy of sixteen and of gargantuan proportions to my medium frame. Renny's size and strength attracted the attentions of the football coach of the Northwest Cougars, the high school Renny would attend if he ever passed the ninth grade, a feat he failed with wide margins in two previous attempts. The coach was spotted drooling in the stands during our football games at the thought of this monster on his team.

Renny Hanks thrived on stuffing kids in lockers and snapping wet towels in the showers with such ferocity the impact would leave a boiling red welt on your legs. His favorite past time was lifting kids into the air by their underwear or jock straps, a feat causing even the bravest of souls to wail like a howler monkey. Even at seventh grade we worried about our future child-bearing abilities. His unkempt mane of greasy brown hair, hooded little eyes and rotten-toothed venomous sneer struck fear into the hearts of his victims. Almost as vicious as Renny was his loyal following of fellow juvenile delinquents who trailed him like a sick pack of rabid dogs.

I hated Renny Hanks with every fiber of my existence. He would hit me, smack me and even spit on me without the slightest provocation on my part. Being somewhat claustrophobic, I shivered with fear anytime I opened my locker. I began to store some of my books and even my coat in other people's lockers because I discovered once Renny set his narrow mind on stuffing you inside the miniature metal coffin, you'd have an easier time catching water in a colander than stopping him, even if it was abundantly clear there wasn't enough room for you inside. Removing the clothes and books made it much less painful.

I'd scoffed at the legendary rumors of his terror-inspiring acts my brother relayed to me when he found out Renny flunked ninth grade again and would be back at Trailridge Junior High. When I first glimpsed Renny, I was astounded at his size, but figured with the number of kids in the school to torture, the odds of him selecting me were miniscule, and I planned to keep those odds in my favor by staying the maximum distance I could from the path of his destruction. However, on the first day of school, I discovered the one thing spotlighting a red bulls-eye on my back. I had something Renny Hanks wanted—Diane.

I escorted Diane to class, walking hand in hand along the beige linoleum hallway, greeting my former grade school chums for the first time in several months. Mike walked behind us with Benny Quinton, the neighborhood Kick the Can champion, arguing with Benny over something having to do with bubblegum, Superman and the Wonder Twins. I didn't pay much attention to their banter because of its stupidity. Diane and I turned the corner leading to the stairwell when we spotted Renny in action in the hallway.

Renny trapped Gill Summers in a headlock, raking his oversized knuckles over Gill's head in the manner of an Indian Rub like he hoped he could set Gill's hair on fire from the friction. Gill tried to scream for help, but each time a sound emanated from his frail little body, Renny rapped his skull and told him to shut up. Renny's entourage egged him on and kept a watchful eye for any approaching teachers. The kids surrounding the spectacle were stuck with the enigma of futilely trying to stop the bullying, or laughing along with Renny and the Boys. It was a difficult choice for most of them because although everyone hates the sight of a little kid getting tortured, it was Gill the Geek and not them. Most of them backed up a sufficient distance so any approaching teacher couldn't frame them as a co-conspirator.

Diane and I edged our way toward the stairwell, caught in the captivating horror of what Renny did to Gill. He may have been a geek, but he was a "sevie" and we knew, at any given moment, we could be standing in his place. I just didn't think I would be standing in his place so quick.

When Renny observed Diane at my side, his mouth twisted into a grin that sent icy shivers down my spine. Dropping Gill Summers like yesterday's garbage, he tromped his way towards us, his intense narrow eyes locked on Diane like a starving lion who gnawed on a scrawny jack rabbit and spotted a wounded antelope in front of him. We were in deep trouble, and I pushed Diane to the stairwell, hoping we could get upstairs before he caught us because the fabled Principal's Office waited at the top of that particular set of stairs. A dreaded place for most youth, it became my sanctuary for the remainder of the school year.

We escaped inside the stairwell without trouble, but the heavy traffic of kids on the stairs put us in dire straits. The door also failed to have a crucial locking mechanism—stupid fire codes. Renny burst through the doorway and trapped us at the bottom of the stairs. The other kids trying to get to class stopped dead in their tracks, a few of the lucky ones at the top managed to

Renny sneered through his rotten teeth at Diane. "Hey, baby. Where you been hiding?"

Diane shuddered with revulsion. Renny's black eyes checked out Diane's blossoming chest through her sweater and licked his chapped lips. In one brave and stupid move, I stepped in front of her. I tried to think of something valiant to say, but all that came to mind was the repeating mantra of "don't die." When Renny's gaze settled on me and his lip curled to a snarl, my testicles shriveled.

"Who the hell are you, dickhead?" he asked through gritted teeth. His breath smelled like a garbage dump on a hot

64

summer day.

"Jack," I said, fear running white hot through my veins as I tilted my head back to meet Renny's glare.

"Jack who?" He poked his meaty finger into my chest. It hurt...a lot.

"Jack Phipps."

"You got a brother named Jake?"

"Yeah, he's my brother."

A shot of hope soared through my trembling frame. For once in my life, Jake might be an asset. Maybe Renny thought Jake was cool and wouldn't break my body in half for his sake. Maybe Renny would pass on Diane since she was the girlfriend of one of his acquaintance's little brother. Those "maybes" darted for the exit with his reply.

"Tell the little punk if he doesn't pay me the five bucks he owes me, I'm gonna rearrange his face."

I grabbed Diane by the arm and pushed her toward the stairs. For a moment, I thought I might make it unscathed.

"I'll tell him when I see him. Thanks."

"Wait a minute, twerp." Renny grabbed my shoulder and pulled me back to the bottom of the stairs. "I ain't done talking to your friend yet."

Renny shoved me hard into the wall, my shoulder taking the brunt of the impact. He moved close to Diane and leaned to her face. She drew back at the halitosis I endured and threw a wide-eyed plea to me for assistance.

"You a hot little thang, ain't ya? What say you and me go to the boiler room, and you can check my tonsils?"

Diane grimaced, whether it was from stench or the corny line spewing from his mouth, I couldn't be sure. What I did know is an unbridled fury boiled in my veins. Images of me jumping between them and beating the crap out of Renny Hanks filled my head. The kids would cheer, his entourage would scramble and Diane would give me a victory kiss. When I jumped in between them and craned my head back to look in Renny's eyes, the victorious image was replaced with one involving me in the intensive care unit with my mom bawling her eyes out over the fact I'd spend the rest of my days in a wheelchair, drinking my meals through a straw and blinking messages to her.

"Leave her alone, Renny." I puffed my skinny chest in a sad attempt to look menacing.

"Or what? What's your little punk ass going to do to me?" A fist the size of a basketball raised in the air, and for one fateful moment I was sure it would descend and crush my skull.

"Mr. Hanks," boomed a resonant voice from the top of the stairs.

Mr. Gashinder, the Vice-Principal scowled at the scene below him. He may as well have worn a halo and a set of wings. Behind him, Mike and Benny positioned themselves at a sufficient distance to avoid implication by Renny. I doubt the moron could fire enough synapses to make the connection anyway. Mr. Gashinder made his way through the crowd gathered on the stairs and inserted himself between me and Renny.

"Is there a problem, Mr. Hanks?"

"No, Mr. Gashinder," Renny mumbled, head hung low. Though Renny was a monster and as tall as our vice-principal, Mr. Gashinder presented a thick, solid mountain of muscle inside a cheap blue suit. Rumor had it he once played defensive back for the Dallas Cowboys and was an ex-Marine. The way Renny retreated solidified in my mind this wasn't their first confrontation.

"Good, then I suggest you get to class. I don't want to hear even a rumor about you today. You got it, mister?"

"Yeah, I got it," Renny said, walking away. When Mr. Gashinder turned his attention to me, Renny backed out the stairwell door. What he mouthed while drawing his index finger across his massive throat was unmistakable. *You're dead.* As Diane and I walked up those stairs, I knew one thing for certain; it would be a long year.

"I guess I should say thanks for getting that creep away from me, Jack," Diane said as we walked home from school. She squeezed my hand, but clenched her jaw as we strolled the sidewalk, passing the homes of our school friends and neighbors, watching them disappear into the doorways one at a time. I could tell by her demeanor some monstrous, soul searching question brewed in those beautiful eyes of hers.

"It was nothin'," I said. I was uncomfortable taking a compliment from people. Compliments were easy enough when you scored a touchdown and slapped some high fives, or hit the game winning dinger in the last inning and the team mauled you at the plate. But, when someone looked me square in the eye and gave a sincere "thanks for the effort" or kudos for the nice work I did, I froze up. I would mumble thank you and try to move the subject on to another topic.

After taking in her furrowed brow, I realized her phrasing wasn't an utterance of gratitude at all. The reason trouble brewed like storm clouds in her eyes and why the temperature dropped several degrees in a matter of seconds was because she was angry. When she got angry, I got nervous. My Uncle Will taught me to listen to not just what a woman says, but how she says it. Even a simple word like "thanks" could be like a blanket over a fire. You couldn't tell if the blanket would extinguish the flame or add more fuel to the blaze. I watched Diane out of the corner of my eye, trying to determine what this particular case would be.

"I thought Renny was going to kill you." Crap. Flame on, call the fire department and put all stations on full alert. The inferno behind her pupils burgeoned, licking at her eyelashes. I had to diffuse this bomb before she exploded. I decided to play up my bravery at the situation.

"Me too. I was pretty scared standing in between you two."

"Then why did you do it?" she asked.

I stopped in my tracks. Her question floored me. Why did I do it? Maybe she'd said something else.

"What did you say?"

"I asked you why you did it. Why did you get between Renny and me?"

"Uh, well…" I sputtered. I was speechless watching my angel with her hands anchored on her hips, a clone of her mother when she was angry. "You looked like you needed help."

"Did I? And you thought you could do something? You thought you'd be Superman, swoop in and carry me away, didn't you? Never mind the other kid was twice your size and has probably already spent time in prison, Jack."

Now my confusion cooked to anger. She was mad because I'd put myself at risk to protect her. I put my life on the line for her, and all she could do was act prissy with her hands on her hips. To top it off, she also thought my efforts were unnecessary and futile. I would have thought a hug and a kiss on the lips for my astounding bravery would have been more appropriate. Now, we stood toe to toe in the middle of the sidewalk questioning my manliness. It was enough to drive a kid insane.

The heat rose in my cheeks. "It worked, didn't it?"

"Because Mr. Gashinder showed up," she said, her volume climbing. "Renny Hanks would have pounded your head in and you know it. I'm not saying it to hurt you, but it's a fact of life you're going to have to deal with pretty quick as you do have to go to school tomorrow. And unless Renny gets arrested between now and then, you're in serious trouble. Why did you do it?"

"Well, what in the hell was I supposed to do?"

Diane's eyes shot wide as her index finger crooked in my face. "You watch your mouth, Jack Phipps." She didn't put up with cursing from me in any form during those days, sounding like my mother when a curse word slipped out. Her parents brainwashed her that cussing was the quickest way to ride down the sinning slide to Hell. She would loosen her standards in a few years, but it forced me to walk the straight and narrow for a while.

"No, seriously, Diane. What was I supposed to do? Let some gorilla maul my girlfriend in the stairwell? Just let him talk to you like that? Is that what I was supposed to do?"

Crimson burned my cheeks, and my hands ached from the clenched tension. Diane crossed her arms with hard eyes and a jutting bottom lip. This was our first serious argument, the first time we'd ever raised our voices to each other.

"Sure, the guy could squash my head like a melon," I continued. "Sure, he could fold me like a friggin' pretzel and shove me in a locker. But, I'll be damned if I'm going to let him walk over my girlfriend. I couldn't. If you wanna chew me out for being stupid with Renny, and for saying friggin' and damned and hell then you go ahead. I'm stickin' by what I did today. I love you too much to let anything happen to you."

I studied Diane's face, trying to read what it told me. Her mask of anger and fury softened the second the last phrase escaped my lips, and I realized I said something right. The words flowed off my tongue like water from a faucet, and I didn't realize what I said until I shut up and rewound the tape recorder in my head and replayed my tirade. Without thinking, the "L" word had slipped out, and I watched the last remnants of her anger wash away. She heard what she wanted, and my last words lingered like a fog in the air. I hoped she wouldn't run away screaming.

"I knew you did," she said at last. "I've been waiting for you say it."

I tried to play it off. "Say what?"

"You know what you said, Jack Phipps. I know what you said."

With a coy giggle, she walked back down the sidewalk. I froze in place, watching her walk away.

Thirty feet away, she spun on her heels and shouted, "I love you, too."

My heart soared, bursting through my chest and sailing into the pink and gold clouds above. Diane and I had been together for a little over four years, and the subject of love didn't come up. It didn't need to. I loved her. She loved me. We both knew it. It's impossible to spend that much time in one another's company without developing feelings one way or the other. If you hated them you left. If you loved them, you stayed and you protected. We loved each other but hadn't said it until now. The sparkle in her eyes, her cherubic face resting underneath her blackened mane, shouting the words "I love you, too" was forever chiseled in a granite image in my head.

Diane crossed a bridge running between the houses spanning the storm drain. The mass of concrete was dry as a bone as we hadn't seen rain for weeks. I caught up to her and took her by the hand. Kids rode their bikes through the ditch under our bridge, whistling and catcalling as they passed.

The world stopped, as if time stood still, and the light from a thousand stars danced in her eyes. She was the most beautiful creature to ever traverse the surface of the earth and she was mine. Like a move I'm sure I watched on television somewhere, I cupped her face in my hands and placed my lips against hers. She responded by throwing her arms around me and kissing me back. For the first time, our tongues escaped the confines of our respective mouths, searching and probing in unknown territory.

Though we pressed together on a concrete bridge spanning a seven-foot ditch which carried away the rain, the minute our lips touched the storm drain dissolved into the beautiful creek running alongside my uncle's farm, and the bridge transformed into my little clubhouse where Diane and I visited last summer. I now did what I hadn't known I'd wanted to do at the time—kissing and holding my young love and hoping the sounds of the world remained silent and the clocks holding this wondrous moment in limbo never started again.

CHAPTER ELEVEN

I steered clear of Renny Hanks for the next couple of days, trying to stay alive until the glorious weekend arrived. The new phenomenon of MTV, the first ever twenty-four-hour music television channel, grew tiresome with the same videos running over and over, so Mike and I made plans to ride our bikes along the storm drain to find out how far we could go. Diane said she had better things to do than go traipsing through a storm drain with a couple of idiots like us. Mike and I took the compliment in stride and rolled down the street with our bikes to start the day's adventure.

The storm drain, which we called "The Creek," ran for miles through the Kansas City neighborhoods. The seven-foot wide expanse of concrete had three-foot-high walls made for carrying away storm water. Though we used the Creek as a large raceway for our bikes, we hadn't followed it more than a mile, turning back when we reached the tunnel leading under the highway. Today would be different.

Mike took his typical lead with his brand new, shiny red Schwinn. It was a true dirt bike. Heavy, a real racing seat and knobby wheels for better traction and skid marks on the concrete. Mike's parents were loving folks but weren't into giving anything for free. He worked his butt off over the last year mowing lawns, shoveling snow and pulling weeds to save for that bike. It was his pride and joy.

I trailed behind him on my crappy little mutt bike, so devoid of any redeeming features its owner threw it to the curb near my dad's office. My dad picked it up, threw it in the trunk and presented it to me as a replacement to my bike, Big Red, which some delinquent stole a week before. When he clapped me on the back and told me a mere coat of paint would make this bike the same as Big Red, I realized he was serious and wanted to cry.

Mike came to a neat, ninety-degree skidding stop at the edge of the hill leading to the Creek. From the top of the hill, the three-foot walls appeared more like ten feet high, and I prayed I didn't pull a Gill. Last month, Gill tried to show off by taking off down the hill and jumping into the creek. He underestimated his speed, was unable to turn and crashed his bike into the opposing wall. I winced at the thought of his testicles being crushed against the handlebars. He broke his ample nose as well as his arm. You almost mustered a modicum of sympathy for the guy. Almost.

"Ready, compadre?" Mike asked.

"Ready, amigo."

We cranked our handlebars as if they were the throttle controls on a real motorcycle. Mike went first, the revving sound reverberating in his throat as I counted down from three. At the word go, he rolled forward and jumped into the creek, twisting his bike in mid-air so it ran parallel to the creek walls, skidding to a stop with a triumphant cry of victory.

"Come on, man. It was awesome. Watch the dip at the end, Jack-o."

I took in the precipice; that six-foot run to the top of the creek wall may well have been length of Niagara Falls. Images of pulling a Gill ran through my head, Mike falling off his bike in great whoops of laughter at my stunt. From the nearby bridge, a conglomeration of my friends from school would point and cut up at my expense. Camera crews from the local television stations would transmit live feeds to the studio of the carnage. I would lay there paralyzed and soaked in a pool of my own blood.

"Come on, man," Mike said. "Sometime this century?"

I blew out air I didn't know I'd held and rolled down the hill, accelerating from zero to Mach 100 in 0.6 seconds. I straddled my bike at the bottom of the hill, poised to leap off the wall into the creek bed, time slogging to a crawl as I went airborne, past the point of no return. I imagined myself as Evel Knieval, the great motorcycle daredevil, to knock back the fear pulsating through my body.

The bed of the Creek was clear, and I twisted my hips to adjust for my requisite trajectory. One inch to the left or right and my brains would end up splattered along the concrete wall. They'd have to use a shovel to scoop me up. I smacked the concrete hard, my wheels threatening to buck me right off the crappy hand-me-down bicycle. I managed to hang on and even throw a decent skid at Mike's side.

I slapped Mike's outstretched palm. "That ruled, man."

"Yeah, totally awesome." Beneath Mike's triumphant grin registered our mutual knowledge we wouldn't try such a moronic stunt again. We rolled along the Creek, ever vigilant for broken glass which would pop our tires or debris that would spill us to the ground.

"Hey, I thought Benny was coming," I said.

"Nah, his mom grounded him. He got bubblegum all

over her new couch, and she wants his head on a chopping block."

"What is it with that kid and bubblegum?" We steered around some brush which accumulated in the creek bed and threw a wave to Judy Yanker's mom who swept her back porch. She yelled something about our need to be careful.

"I don't know," Mike said. "It's like he's obsessed with it or something. Even tried to tell me Superman couldn't break out of a bubblegum bubble laced with kryptonite."

"What? That's the stupidest thing I've ever heard."

"No shit," Mike said. "Next thing I know, I'm arguin' with the moron about it."

"That's the same argument you had on the first day of school when King Renny almost ripped my head off."

"The very one. When he brought up the Wonder Twins and their stupid monkey, I told him to shut up. Speaking of Renny, looks like you've survived another week."

We rode in silence for a moment, bunny hopping over fallen branches, riding up the sidewalls of the creek if they happened to release from their perpendicular confines and throw us a slope. I thought back over the week and Mike's comment of my survival. Another week of school and I'd survived. Is this how I would live for the rest of the year? Running from class to class in the hopes I wouldn't run into Renny Hanks? Sending scouts ahead to check if the coast was clear so I could at least walk to class with my girlfriend without the fear of dying? Was this my destiny or could I do something about it?

"I hate that monkey," I said, tendrils of anger taking hold. "I wish he'd leave me alone."

"No way that's happening, my friend," Mike said.

"Yeah, but I can hope, can't I? I don't know what to do about him and Diane."

"What can you do? He wants her. She hates him. Case closed."

I huffed. "No, case closed in her mind. She thinks telling him off will get him to leave her alone. But, I've seen the way he looks at her, the way he licks his lips and checks out her boobs. He's an animal."

We rounded a large curve, concentrating on the debris of bottles and empty beer cans laying in front of us. Someone liked to use this as a party spot.

"That's an insult to animals. He's a full-fledged douche," Mike said.

"I wish I had an ounce of muscle or could do some karate action. I'd kick Renny Hanks' stupid, fat ass into next week."

Mike and I laughed at the sentiment but silenced at the unmistakable eyesore fifteen yards ahead of us. Perched on the bridge atop a bicycle much too diminutive for his gargantuan frame, Renny Hanks waited like a hawk along with his gang of future inmates. Oh, we were dead. We were so dead.

CHAPTER TWELVE

The bottle flew from Renny's hand at the speed of light, humming as air caught the bottle opening. Fortunately, Renny's aim wasn't as good as his velocity, and the bottle shattered at a harmless distance in front of our bikes.

The crash of glass broke us from the initial shock, and our feet wailed on the bike pedals as Renny clamored down the bank with his bike lifted over his head.

"Is he back there?" Mike asked a minute later, concentrating on the cluttered path ahead of us.

My chest heaved and lungs burned. "Yeah, he was at the Creek when we turned the corner."

"He can move pretty good for a fat ass."

We were both well aware of what would happen if Renny and his crew caught us in the drainage ditch. This section of the Creek ran near the highway where the houses were sparse and farther from the road. The mouth to the Death Tunnel running under the highway lay straight ahead, ready to gobble us both.

The Death Tunnel was a piece of local lore. Legend had it one of the neighborhood kids died in this part of the ditch, drowning while playing during a rain storm. They found his limp, water-logged body inside this tunnel, wedged under a piece of peeled back sheet metal. Kids said his ghost haunted this tunnel, waiting for other kids to come through to join him.

"The Tunnel?" Mike asked, nodding toward the entrance fifty yards ahead.

Over my shoulder, I couldn't spot Renny but knew he barreled our way. His curses lifted and carried on the westerly breeze.

"Think Renny'll go in after us?" I asked.

"If he can get his fat ass through the opening," Mike yelled over his shoulder. I marveled at his bravado. Mike was the brave one of our duo, always spitting in the face of danger.

"I heard that, punk," Renny's voice shouted from behind us. "I'm gonna kick both your asses."

The mouth of the tunnel drew close. A local kid really did drown in the Creek ten years ago, but I didn't know if they found his body in this tunnel. Even though I knew his ghost wasn't haunting the place, it was still wet, dark and long. Stretching a good quarter of a mile, the opening on the other side of the highway was nothing but a pinpoint of light. We slowed as we hit the entrance, assessing as best we could the obstacles laying before us, the fact we'd never mustered the courage to enter the Tunnel looming large.

Mike squinted into the blackness, breathing heavy. "What do you think?"

"Let's go," I said, stealing one last glance over my shoulder.

"You sure?"

"What choice do we have?" I pedaled my bike into the darkness, the temperature dropping as the tunnel swallowed the sunlight.

Behind us, Renny skid to a halt at the entrance to the

tunnel. His moronic gang of derelicts tried to stop and crashed into their leader. The comedic pileup knocked Renny off his bike, but he stayed on his feet cursing. The rest of the idiots lay behind him in a mess of limbs and rusted metal.

"Come on, Mike," I whispered. "We can put some distance between us and them."

Mike's voice echoed off the dark wall. "I'm waiting for your pokey ass to get out of my way."

We continued in silence, our tires squelching through the muck and Renny's voice making more than enough noise for the entire group. He insisted he would pummel us, kick our ass, twist us into pretzels and a few other choice promises whose language and sexual nature forbid me listing them here. All that mattered was they continued their chase. The end of the tunnel approached, and once we cleared it we would escape and live to cower another day. Just as hope loomed eternal, a distinctive pop emanating from my front tire shattered my confidence.

"Oh shit." I shimmied my handlebars, trying to turn my sluggish front tire. I had a flat.

"Move it, Jack. You're slowing down."

"I think I got a flat, Mikey," I said.

"You what? You sure?"

"I'm sure. Keep going, we'll see how far it'll take us."

My legs pumped a whirlwind, muscles aching, oblivious to the obstacles laying in our path. I was in serious, serious trouble—a flat tire on my bike in an unknown neighborhood with a pack of murderous thieves hot on my tail. Mike caught me in the tunnel, watching my front wheel wobble back and forth as my speed dropped along with my control. The tunnel exit loomed twenty yards away.

"We'll ditch your bike around the corner, above the creek wall and keep going on mine," Mike said. "We should be able to stay ahead of them."

I shook my head as I struggled with the handlebars. "It'll never work. They'll catch us."

"Then what? What in the hell are we going to do?"

The second I uttered the words "it'll never work" an image flashed through my brain. Mike and I on the floor of my living room in the wee hours of the morning watching a ton of movies we weren't supposed to watch. Cable television was something new to the Phipps' house over the last year, and I discovered the wonderment of the female flesh airing around two o'clock in the morning.

But, the images flashing across my brain weren't of naked women, but the cheesy war movie from last week. The Nazi's were closing fast, overwhelming the American defensive line. Two soldiers, buddies since they were five, lay on the ground firing round after round into the onslaught of German soldiers. One of the buddies catches one in the shoulder. As they attempt to retreat, he catches another slug in the leg. Unable to continue, he begs his friend to go on without him, to leave him and save himself. Mike and I both commented how that wouldn't happen in real life. Yet, here we were, faced with the exact same scenario, albeit without the flying bullets, but life and death all the same. I couldn't believe I was going to say it.

"Mike, go on without me."

"Are you crazy? Renny'll kick your face into next week."

My progress slowed, the wheel rim slipping along the empty innertube. Mike hung close by on his two good tires, but Renny closed in. A sharp curve loomed up ahead.

"Well, better me than both of us," I said. "I'll think of something. Get out of here."

"What are you going to do?"

My mind raced at the possibilities. I wished I could conjure a sharp stick or maybe a bat with some nails sticking out of it that I could scare Renny away with. Even better would be a Molotov cocktail. I would stand in the middle of the creek, bare chested and buff with a lighter in one hand and the kerosene soaked rag in the other, daring Renny to come closer. A third possibility consisting of me abandoning the creek and hiding in the nearby bushes sounded more feasible.

"Around the bend, I'll pull the bike out of the creek and hide. You keep going to draw Renny away. I'll start back toward home, and you hook up with me when you lose him. Sound good?"

"Dude," Mike said. "That sucks. I'm the bait and you get away."

"You have a better suggestion? Give me your bike and I'll pedal off into the sunset while you hide like a chicken."

"No, thanks," Mike said. "I'd rather run than sit and hope the giant moron doesn't see me."

I threw my bike over the three-foot wall of the creek and clambered up. Mike lingered in the creek as if this were the last time we'd ever lay eyes upon each other. The whoops and shouts from Renny and his goons echoed through the tunnel, growing louder by the second.

"You'd better get going, Mikey," I said.

"Goliath's comin'. You'd better find a cave to hide in, David."

I blinked in surprise that Mike Washington knew a biblical

story. The farther he pedaled away, the deeper the panic dug its claws in my gut. The bringer of my demise would round the bend any second, and I had nowhere to hide.

Scanning the yard, I took in the trees, flower beds, and a promising hedge running in front of a scarred wooden fence leading to a brown ranch house. I didn't know if I'd be able to make the hedge before Renny and his goons rounded the corner, but I would sure try. Picking up the bike, I sprinted toward the bushes, the gang's mindless prattle announcing their arrival as they rounded the curve. I wasn't going to make it. I was dead.

With a desperate heave, I threw my bike over the hedge where it cracked against the wooden privacy fence, the sound of the impact echoing like a shotgun blast across the Grand Canyon. I followed the path of my bike and dove in after it, stealing a last glance over my shoulder to glimpse Renny's face rounding the curve of the creek. I crashed to the bottom of the hedge, the branches scratching my face and cracking under the strain of my weight. My salvation rested on a hope the idiot pack yelled at each other too loud to hear me. I pressed my face in the dirt, unmoving and praying.

"Whoa, whoa," Renny said. "What was that?"

"What was what, Renny? Come on, they're gonna get away."

"Shut up, dumbass," Renny said. "Up there, in the bushes. I thought I saw something."

My heart stopped and I couldn't breathe, like someone knocked the air out of me. I'd been spotted. Pretty soon they'd quit talking about it and come to investigate. They'd find me, drag me to the creek and kill me. The last sounds anyone would hear would be my desperate screams for mercy and tennis shoes dragging through the dry earth in protest of their direction.

"I'm gonna check it out," Renny said. I lay still, eyeing the ground in front of my face, afraid to even breathe. The thought of jumping to my feet and running flashed through my mind, but fear paralyzed my limbs.

"Hey, you morons! You gonna stand there with your thumbs up your asses or what?"

The melodic voice of Michael Allen Washington floated across the fall breeze, as welcome as Luciano Pavarotti would be to an opera lover. It was the sound of the wind against Superman's cape to Lois Lane as she dangled from a cliff. It was Mikey coming back to save my butt and draw the goons away. It was the bravest act of heroism I would ever witness.

"There's that Washington punk. Get him."

Renny's crew screamed bloody murder among a cacophony of rattling chains and metal fenders as they scrambled back on their bikes and took off after Mike. I waited until their shouts faded, exhaled my relief and climbed back to my feet. Before I could clear the top of the hedge, however, a meaty paw clamped on the back of my shirt and sent me airborne, flying across the backyard and crashing to the ground.

"I thought you was hiding back there," Renny said, advancing on me. "Get up. Come on, kick my fat ass, you little twerp."

Renny towered over me, and I sprawled helpless on the grass. I tried scrambling away, walking backward like a crab until I knocked my head against a large oak tree. Renny bent over and grabbed fistfuls of my shirt collar, lifting my face square with his, my feet dangling a full foot off the ground.

"You've made fun of me for the last time, dick brain. Any

last words before I rip off your face?"

In great moments of danger, when faced with ultimate peril and impending demise, an individual's true character emerges. When placed in a similar situation, some people would remain speechless, unable to form even the simplest words or phrases. Others would beg and plead, soiling themselves in the hopes their tormentor would take pity and let them live to see another day. Before this moment, I would have laid money I would take the latter path, but I surprised myself and did the most unwise thing I could have possibly done.

"Go screw yourself, Renny." I hawked a thick wad of phlegm and spit it in his face. Watching his face contort in confused anger as my spittle dripped across his nose to his bulbous, cracked lips made whatever retribution I was due worth it.

His confusion exploded to fire, the rapid intake of oxygen from his heaving chest fanning the flames. He drew back his massive fist, ready to split open my skull against this tree. My once brave mind realized Renny wouldn't just beat me up. He would kill me this day for real. I'm talking the dead, pulverized body of a thirteen-year-old seventh grader found beaten to death beside a storm drain in a Shawnee neighborhood. Renny Hanks was capable of it, and, judging from the fury in his face, I had no doubt in my mind that murder, cold-blooded murder, was the exact emotion dominating his pea brain. I watched his fist draw back, reach its apex and hitch, ready to spring forward. I closed my eyes and waited for it.

"I don't think that would be a smart idea, Mr. Hanks," a familiar voice said behind Renny. I cracked my eyes in time to notice Renny spin around, still clutching me by the shirt and face the intervener. I exhaled with relief at the voice's owner.

"This ain't none of your damn business," Renny said, his teeth clenched with such force I heard the enamel grinding.

"Well, I'm making it my business. Put Mr. Phipps down. Right now," Mr. Gashinder said. How or why Mr. Gashinder happened to be there at that particular moment in time, I cared not.

"Or what? We ain't on school property."

Mr. Gashinder wore a pair of worn gray sweatpants and a thin white t-shirt with the initials USMC stamped in bold black on the front. His massive arms, by day hidden beneath his cheap suits, bulged like immense boulders, tense and ready for action. The sun bounced off his shaven head and stubble covered his cheeks, like Mr. Clean having a bad day, and I was glad he was on my side.

"No, Mr. Hanks, you are not on school property. You are on my property. This is my yard. And, I suggest you let Mr. Phipps go this instant."

"Or what, dickhead?"

Oh, did my spirits soar when the corners of Mr. Gashinder's mouth broke upward, the years of frustration Renny Hanks caused this man etched in his face. He couldn't touch Renny in the school, but while Renny trespassed on his own property while threatening the life of another student? The phrase justifiable homicide floated through my young brain.

Whatever the effect of Mr. Gashinder's words on Renny, he dropped me. I scrambled to my feet and ran to the side of my savior thinking Renny would make his way to the creek to join the rest of his crew with his tail between his legs. Instead, he stood like a defiant statue, ready for battle. He took a hesitant step toward Mr. Gashinder. He was even stupider than I thought.

"I'm sick of you, Gashinder." Renny spit on the ground for effect.

"Not as much as I am of you, Mr. Hanks," Mr. Gashinder said, smooth as silk. They glared at each other for a moment before Mr. Gashinder craned his head a few degrees in my direction. "Jack, I think you'd better go on home now."

"But, Mr. Gashinder, I want to stay and...."

"No, Jack. I don't think you need to see this. I suggest you get on your bike and go on home. Mr. Hanks and I have a few things to settle."

Renny glared as I walked back toward the hedge. I wrestled my bike out of the bushes and wheeled it back toward the two giants. I paused, wanting to stay and watch. Mr. Gashinder's hands opened and closed at his sides, a mere two feet from Renny.

"Go home, Jack," Mr. Gashinder said without taking his eyes off Renny. I made my way toward the street, away from the creek. As I reached his house, I sprinted around to the opposite side. I wouldn't miss this battle for a million dollars.

When I reached the other side and crawled around the corner, the two still talked. Well, Mr. Gashinder talked in a low, calm voice. Renny's nostrils flared in response. I reflected how some kind of guardian angel must have forced my hand and caused me to land in the yard of the one person in the world who could have saved me from Renny Hanks. It was a true miracle. I continued to watch and when the talking across the yard ended, I held my breath. I didn't tell Mr. Gashinder I stayed, nor did we ever discuss the situation in the future. I lay in hiding, lips curled upward at the misfortune of my foe, and thanking the good Lord above my name wasn't Renny Hanks at that particular moment in time.

CHAPTER THIRTEEN

Junior high flew by like a hot rod on a drag strip, burning the pavement with trash and swirls of leaves floating through its wake. That's what I felt like. The hot rod was time, and I was the debris behind the car, floating and tumbling.

We made it through endless, nauseating renditions of Toni Basil's "Mickey," dialed Jenny at 867-5309 countless times and tried to look as cool as possible in our Member's Only jackets while playing Hacky Sack outside the school. While the world witnessed the assassination of Ghandi and Reagan kicking the crap out of Walter Mondale in the Presidential election like a narc at a biker rally, we immersed ourselves in the Miami Vice dress fad of light jackets and loafers without socks. A lot of crazes came and went, but yet here I stood ready to close my locker for the last time in junior high. The next time I opened a locker, it would be at Shawnee Mission Northwest High School, home of the Cougars.

I stopped in the hall laden with loose papers strewn from emptied notebooks. Kids walked around, arms looped over each other's shoulders, pointing out the inane comments written in their yearbooks. I removed the pictures taped inside my locker, my last act before I went home.

The first one I fingered featured me, Benny, and Mike in our football jerseys by the goal post trying to look mean, Diane lying on the ground in front of me, striking a seductive pose in her cheerleader uniform next to Benny and Mike's girlfriends. I stared hard at Diane's picture, astounded how much her physique changed over the last few years.

Her long, once curly, dark hair hung straight, draped over her shoulder with her bangs curled under. Her face, once cherubic and round, elongated under sharp cheekbones with a complexion as smooth as silk. Thick eyelashes set off her still icy-blue irises. Her body—oh, how her body grew up. It was now the epitome of perfection, and if she shaped up any better I think my head would explode. Though a mere fifteen, she would give the Pope whiplash if he saw her in a bikini.

The next picture featured Mike and I at Worlds of Fun in front of the Scream Roller, one of the first roller coasters to rotate upside down. Strapped in a chair secure enough to send you to the moon, we climbed two hundred feet in the air then plummeted to the bottom at 55 miles per hour before rolling through two upside-down loops. The whole ride was over in thirty seconds, something of a gyp considering the typical sixty-minute wait in line to get on the stupid thing. Mike and I rode the roller coaster twelve times in a row that hot summer afternoon when the lines were short, and I admit you noticed the green around our gills in the photo.

A third picture showed me and Mr. Gashinder, his thick hand resting on my shoulder after a long evening cleaning the offices for Secretary's Day. He'd recruited me for the cleanup, and we'd scrubbed, filed, and dusted so the women in the office would be in for a heck of a surprise the next morning. It wasn't exciting work, but I owed Mr. Gashinder for taking care of Renny Hanks for me. If I doubted if the near-death experience with Renny ever happened, I only had to look at the scar on Mr. Gashinder's middle knuckle from his fist meeting Renny's crooked teeth to prove it.

Renny Hanks left me alone after the "Creek Incident." He'd missed school for a week and a half before returning with some faded bruises around the eyes and mouth and his right arm in a sling as if a truck plowed him over. He told the school a group of six boys jumped and managed to overcome him after he'd taken out four of them. Myself, Mike, Diane, Mr. Gashinder and, of course, Renny himself knew different. He gave me a wide berth and didn't utter a word to any of my crew again. I think he feared we'd blow his cover.

On his second attempt, Renny graduated the ninth grade and left for Northwest High School. He played football for Coach Utt for half a year before getting kicked out of too many games for kneeing other players and one official in the groin. Three weeks later, he got expelled from the school for drug possession and for threatening some kid with a switchblade.

The last few things on the locker door were clips of articles I'd written for the school newspaper. I found I liked to write, and Mr. Hawkins said I showed promise. If I could combine the writing with my Uncle Will's talent of spinning a yarn, I figured I might be able to pass myself off as an author someday.

I folded the columns around the pictures and put them in my backpack. Reaching into the back of the locker, I grabbed the rest of the love notes Diane wrote me over the last few weeks and lay them on top of yearbook in my bag. Zipping the backpack, I shut the door to the locker, listening to the sound echo in the empty hallway. Diane waited a few lockers over, leaning against the doors, watching me.

"What are you doing?" I asked.

She flirted with me as she always did. "Watching you. Do you mind?"

"Nah, I don't mind. I thought you'd be sick of looking at me by now."

"Don't think I ever will be." She leaned over and kissed me. "Walk me home, handsome?"

"God, you're so corny," I said, draping my arm around her shoulder and tugging her along the hall.

She rested her head on my shoulder. "Yeah, well you're ugly, but you don't hear me complaining."

"Make up your mind. Am I ugly or handsome?"

"No comment. I'll make you think about it for a while."

At the exit doors, we turned around, taking in the empty halls that held us in check for three years.

"Will you miss this rathole?" I asked.

"A little, but, I think I'm ready for the big time. How 'bout you?"

"As long as I've got you, I'm ready for anything."

Together we walked out the front doors to the junior high, placing our palm prints on the glass doors one last time. As those doors clicked shut behind us, a chapter of our lives closed. Sure, we were only fifteen, but I could already feel the wheels of time accelerating, gaining velocity at an exponential rate. High school would begin in a few months, followed by college, a job, a house, kids, et cetera, et cetera. My dad always said life would become a blur, and I would stop and wonder where it went. I finally understood what he meant. Diane's eyes swept the sky with a content close-lipped smile, and I squeezed her tight as we walked away from the school. It was 1984.

CHAPTER FOURTEEN

In the summer of 1984, I grew tired of finding nothing in my pockets but lint and entered the job market. Mike and I rode our bikes all over town trying to land a cool job, one paying decent wages with cool people who could lead us to parties. Mike's aspirations ran more along the lines of hot women having dumped his latest girlfriend of the week in search of the bluer skies that summer days at the pool or the right job could bring.

Unfortunately, we started our job hunt too late, and everywhere we looked was already overstocked with pimple plagued teens slopping burgers and fries, washing cars or stocking shelves in the supermarket. I worried about landing a job at all, much less one where Mike and I could work together. Fortunately, fate was on our side one hot June afternoon. Sitting on the curb outside of the Bronze Café, a Mexican-American restaurant, Mike and I debated about applying for jobs.

"It says they're hiring," I said.

Mike's mouth curled down. "I already talked to Phil and Judy who tried to get jobs here. The guy said no waiting experience, no job."

"Maybe we could be cooks or something instead of waiters."

"And take a job without tips?"

"It could be worse. We could be garbage men or something."

Mike shook his head in protest. "But, tips are where the money is."

"Screw tips, Washington. I'd settle for anything to get my old man off my back and my ass off this bicycle seat."

As if on cue, the back door flew wide and two, skinny Hispanic guys stumbled through the opening. They yelled in Spanish at the person who'd shoved them through the door. Their hands and arms were a blur of obscene gestures returned with vigor by a fat old guy with a gut drooping well below his beltline. After a minute of colorful exchanges, the two men climbed into a rusty jalopy and burned rubber out of the parking lot, leaving a cloud of black dust in their wake. Mike and I watched them peel off from our bikes.

"You kids deaf or something?" Fat Guy asked, sunlight dancing from his chrome dome.

We squinted against the sunlight toward the open doorway. The bald guy with the grease-covered apron and meaty, tattooed forearms was talking to us.

"Who us?" I said.

"No, the other two little punks hanging around my back door. What the hell are you doing here?"

I hopped off my bike. "We're looking for jobs, sir." My dad told me to address strangers as sir. You couldn't go wrong with being respectful.

"Sir, eh? I like you boys. You want to be Hobart Engineers in my place, eh?"

I thought the guy was kidding. Engineers? Us? How old

94

did he think we were? My dad complained about the engineers at his construction sites and how "they couldn't find their asses with both hands and a flashlight." I had no idea what a Hobart Engineer was or why they'd need an engineer in a little Mexican restaurant, but I figured it must pay pretty well even if it represented a ground floor position.

"Yes, sir. When can we start?" I said.

"Jack," Mike whispered. "What are you doing?"

"Getting us cool jobs, now shut up."

Fat Man waved us inside. Mike trudged behind in protest until he reached the kitchen of the restaurant and set eyes on the cute teenage waitresses. He was in like flint when one of the cute ones winked at him.

He rubbed his hands together. "Where do we start?"

"Right there," Fat Man said, pointing to our left at the piles of dishes on the floor, on the sink, in the sink, on the shelves, everywhere. "Four dollars and fifty cents an hour. I throw in a free hamburger for each of you if you start right now."

Four-fifty an hour was a generous wage for a kid back then, especially since we encountered so much trouble finding any job in the first place. Bargain Barn offered a paltry three fifty, and I would have to work not only with Jake, but under his supervision. Mike eyeballed the waitress who winked at him earlier before waggling his eyebrows at me.

"Good," Fat Man said. "You Engineers better get busy. We got lots of plates to clean."

I think back on the first day at the restaurant with great fondness. We experienced some great times there, and made new friends along with some decent cash. I asked Fat Man why he called us Hobart Engineers, but he wouldn't say. The following day, the Hobart brand dishwasher answered my question. Like a moron, I understood Fat Man's joke.

All summer long, Mike and I toiled in the hot, humid dish room of the restaurant, flinging plates and silverware around like nobody's business. As crappy as the job was, and as grungy as we would emerge after a long day, being a Hobart Engineer was the best job I ever had.

CHAPTER FIFTEEN

It was utter torture waiting for the Van Halen calendar on the wall of my room to turn to July 2, 1985. My sixteenth birthday and I sat on top of the world. I wouldn't get the fabled car, this much I knew. My folks weren't stupid like Laura Dunnsberry's parents who bought her a brand new convertible Mustang for her sweet sixteenth. She got two speeding tickets and totaled the car inside of three weeks. Even though I wouldn't have my own car, I was still sixteen and could now drive.

I even cajoled my father into taking off work early so he could haul me to the driver's license bureau to nab my ticket to freedom. He didn't think I was ready or had spent enough time behind the wheel. But, he relied on his recollections of our previous driving escapades together and didn't include my practice time with Mom. As the tester and I drove away, my dad's worry-crunched face flashed in the rearview mirror as if he bid farewell to his car in one piece.

During the test, I was a master. I kept a careful eye on the speedometer wavering a mile per hour below the posted speed limit. I signaled with precision at turns as if the required one hundred feet lit up like a neon strip in the road. I conducted shoulder checks at lane changes, ensuring I didn't goose the powerful V-8 of the Buick too much or slam on the brakes too hard—an egg could have balanced on the hood of the car. I even managed to parallel park like I'd been doing it for thirty years. But, as we pulled back into the lot, I spied the obvious relief painting my father's face, and I knew my solo driving time would be limited. Still, I scored the license, and on the way home it burned a hole in my wallet, screaming for use. I could hope my father would fall asleep and Mom would cave in.

Once home, to celebrate the monumental occasion of my birth, my mother baked my favorite chocolate cake with chocolate icing. The cake would follow my favorite dinner fare of fried cubed steak, breaded with a ton of garlic, mashed potatoes and gravy, and the sweetest tasting corn one could ever hope to cross the palate. I over-gorged myself on the main course, but managed to fill in the sparse cracks in my stomach with a healthy slice of chocolate cake.

Presents followed dinner with the usual clothes my mother thought would suit me, but rarely did, and cassette tapes of rock bands who already flamed out after burning as bright as a supernova for one hit or two. I did manage to score a portable cassette player from Dad which stunned me for my father reserved the extravagant gifts for Christmas. My brother gave me Van Halen's 1984 album, a generous gift from him.

Diane came over an hour after the family party ended while we laid around in the living room, moaning with hands draped over extended bellies. She joined us in front of the television, as comfortable in front of my family as she would be in front of her own. When a commercial interrupted the newest episode of Miami Vice, my father broke the silence.

"Jack, why don't you show Diane what you got today?"

My mind went blank and I scrambled to recall the cool

present which would mean something to Diane. Images of jeans and shirts flashed through my brain along with overplayed sounds of Journey and Boston. Did he mean the cassette player? Dad noted my blank expression and came to my rescue.

"Your driver's license, Braniac," he said.

Embarrassed, I extracted the license from my Velcro wallet and handed it to Diane. It was the best license picture I would ever take.

She held the license by the edges as if afraid she'd smear it. "Cool, Jack. Was the test hard?"

"Nah, piece of cake. The instructor said I was one of the most careful drivers he'd ever been with."

Out of the corner of my eye, I glanced at my father, sure he knew the instructor said no such thing. The old geezer said nothing to me during the test except when to turn and to watch out for the kids crossing the street. He checked off whatever lay on his clipboard list which made me nervous because I couldn't tell if a check was a good thing or bad. I hoped Dad would take the bait and let me go for a drive. Though I figured my chances were as good as my brother graduating from high school, I gave it a shot. Imagine my surprise when my father spoke again.

"Why don't you take her for a spin, Jack?"

My head whipped around in time to catch the smile sliding across my father's face as he reached into his pocket for the keys. Out of the corner of my eye, Jake's jaw slapped against his chest. Dad hadn't give him the keys to his car in the year and a half since he'd scored his license. When Jake begged, my father said he'd rather croak from a heart attack in the driveway than let Jake drive him to the hospital. When he tossed the keys in my direction, the light gleaming off the metal as the key ring spun through the air and floated into my hand, it was his way of letting me know he trusted me. With the keys to his most prized possession on the planet in hand, a lump seized my throat.

"Thanks, Pop," I said.

As Diane and I approached the garage door, an unwelcome sense of fear crept into my bones. After all, once on the road there would be nobody there to save me but myself. I might forget how to park or when to flip a turn signal. The image of the local police tailing me, waiting for me to screw up so they could issue my death warrant in the way of a ticket, haunted me. One little ticket would be an instant end to my driving career. Images of ambulances, jail cells, and flashing lights blinded me. I resisted the urge to toss the keys back to my dad and saying no thanks, too much responsibility for me, Pop.

Diane's comforting hand on my shoulder cast those images away. This was my night, something I'd anticipated since my Uncle Will let me steer the tractor so many years ago. I'd be free to cruise the streets of Kansas City unabated. I could crank up the stereo, drop the windows and howl at the moon if I so chose. Diane and I could find a quiet spot in a nearby park and explore each other's tonsils without the fear of my brother lurking about in the hope of catching us in the act. An awesome sense of adventure surged through my veins, and I was as excited to get behind the wheel as I'd been when we'd made the trek to the license bureau.

My father called out after us. "Jack? Be back by nine and put back whatever gas you use up."

"No problem." Relief swam through me that I might be spared some sort of lecture on being careful. I'd seen enough of the films in Driver's Ed and undergone tortuous counseling sessions by both parents.

He then squashed any hopes of having fun with his baby. "And if you wreck it, just keep driving."

His solemn warning released the panicky butterflies. I'd heard him say it to Jake with regard to my mother's car and he meant it. If I wrecked his baby, I would indeed have to keep driving—maybe to Florida or up to Canada. Out of the country would be better than what I would have to face at home if I put so much as a scratch on his car.

"Gotcha, Dad. I'll be careful."

Escaping the living room, Diane and I slipped into the garage and stopped, gaping at the monstrous Buick before us. With its keys in my possession, it appeared as long as a cruise ship, the massive hood like jaws waiting to spring open and swallow us whole. Though a horrific shade of burned chocolate, it shined and sparkled from the fresh coat of wax Dad applied.

This was the first nice car he'd owned. We'd driven a plethora of cars in the past, going through them like the State of Kansas had a law on the books that residents must possess a worthless piece of junk that blew a gasket every hundred miles. With the new job, Dad bought this massive brown boat I was sure could pull a couple of skiers behind it and still hold twelve of your closest friends inside in comfort. I was nervous as hell, but Diane once again put her hand on my shoulder.

"Come on, Jack. Take me for a spin."

Minutes later we cruised the streets of Overland Park as cool as we could be. We cranked KY102 and jammed to Led Zepplin, Ratt and Quiet Riot, honking and waving at the few of our friends who were old enough to drive or knew somebody that did. It was Saturday night, man, and Metcalf, the cruising strip for the kids of Johnson County, was packed. The air stank of burnt rubber and cigarette smoke and sounded of a cacophony of rock-n-roll tunes blaring from blown-out speakers. Diane sported a grin of utter contentment, matching my own feelings at the moment. We just drove, without a care about where we went or if we ever arrived. It was one of the greatest moments of my life until the car in the neighboring lane blared its horn.

"Hey, look at this," the familiar voice said. "A pussy and his skank in Daddy's car."

I groaned, recognizing the voice and craned my head to take in the drunk face of Renny Hanks. It had been a long time since our last encounter, but it wasn't long enough. He rode shotgun in a beat-up Mustang with the dents and scratches of a demolition derby sacrifice. The long-haired derelict behind the wheel shot me a sneer below his narrowed eyes, a joint resting between his slimy lips.

"What are you looking at, Phipps? Huh?"

The hatred for me on Renny's face blasted like a neon light. I prayed for the light to flip green so we could get out of there.

"You too good to talk to me, you little piece of shit?"

"Look, Renny," I said, hoping my voice wasn't quaking. "I don't want any trouble. Come on, man, it's my first night out. Trouble is the last thing we want."

Renny's face froze and I could imagine the mouse on the wheel inside his thick skull churning away, trying to generate enough juice to get his dope-laden synapses firing. I thought for a brief moment he might give it up and drive away with his druggy friend. Instead, he flicked his cigarette against the side of the old man's car and threw his beer can, spraying the half-full contents across the blacktop.

"No trouble, Phipps? I think that's exactly what you found."

Renny opened the car door and swung his tree trunk legs out. Before he could clear the door, the traffic light turned green. The adrenaline coursing through my body concentrated itself in my right foot, and I floored the Buick, lighting up the already noisy night with the screeching sound of rubber spinning on asphalt. When the tires found purchase, the Buick shot forward and sped through the intersection. The rearview mirror showed the Mustang whip behind us, flash its brights, and begin gaining ground. The chase was on.

CHAPTER SIXTEEN

"This ain't no game, son," my father said during my first driving lesson. We crept along the tree-lined thoroughfare through our neighborhood. I studied his every move from the passenger seat, ready to mimic them to perfection if given the opportunity.

"The key to driving," he continued, "is to watch out for the morons whose sole purpose in life is to try to run you off the road."

I thought he joked, but his face reflected utter seriousness. My father was renowned throughout the land for the verbal abuse he could issue upon the other drivers on the road. Mom slipped once and told me Dad once kept a gun in the car. Having witnessed how he flipped from Jekyll to Hyde once someone cut him off or tailgated him, I was thankful she convinced him to get rid of it. I thought the gun might be hidden somewhere in the house, but I wasn't about to go looking for it.

"Gotcha, Pop," I said.

"I'm serious, Jack. I remember how I used to drive when I was a teen-ager and if I ever catch you pulling some of the stunts I pulled, I'll skin you alive. You drive like that in the city and you'll be eating a phone pole for your next meal."

It was a corny analogy, but effective. My dad showed me the country roads in central Nebraska where he and Uncle Will once lit up the blacktop. Taking some of those curves at sixty miles per hour made your hair stand on end. The thought of the same turn at a hundred, the speeds my father related he and Uncle Will used to travel, made you want to wet yourself.

"Don't worry, Dad. I'll be careful."

"You'd better. This isn't a game sitting behind the wheel of the car. Your life can change in the blink of an eye."

Instead of blinking, I rolled my eyes at the phrase. He'd said it a gazillion times since I'd first broached the subject of driving. I heard it when we climbed into the car, when we witnessed a person getting a ticket, when there was a wreck on the six o'clock news and even in my sleep, when I dreamed of racing through the streets. However, while he gave "the game" speech, the wisest course of action was to remain stoic and turn into a bobble head doll.

After a couple miles, he pulled to a side street, put the car in park and stared at me. I didn't blink or give any sign he might perceive as weakness. He searched for any chinks in my armor to exploit, giving him the excuse to keep me from behind the wheel. My resolve won out the moment as he climbed out and motioned for me to slide over behind the wheel. I chewed the inside of my cheeks to contain my enthusiasm, careful to avoid displaying any sign of enjoyment. This wasn't a game and I wouldn't treat it as such.

Once on the road I drove like my grandmother, slow and decisive, determined to show a steady hand and a keen eye. I checked my mirrors as instructed during Driver's Ed and kept a close eye on the speedometer. Though going a few miles under the speed limit, I'm sure Dad still thought I went too fast. He said nothing, maintaining a white-knuckle grip on the armrest. He wasn't enjoying this at all.

"Jesus," I said, my heartrate doubling when a Camaro barreled behind me, going at least sixty in the thirty mile per hour zone. Dad whipped his head around and shot daggers at the teenage driver behind us who responded with a blaring horn and constant flashing of his bright lights. I was sure he would ram me, but he maintained a distance inches from my rear bumper.

"What do I do, Dad?" Panic crept in and wet my palms. "Do I speed up, pull over, what?"

"What do you think? You're behind the wheel."

"Shouldn't I slow down like you do when somebody's tailgating you?"

"Spoken like a true prodigy," he said, much to my surprise. My dad's strategy in situations such as this was to slow to a crawl which tended to further infuriate the driver behind him. It was effective on the highway and a victory when he boxed the other driver in.

So, I did as my father would. I let off the gas and alternated my attention between the view of the Camaro's grill in the rearview mirror and the descending speedometer needle. The horn on the Camaro changed from an intermittent honk to a constant blare. After a clearing opened in the oncoming traffic, the kid gunned the engine and swerved around us, whipping by on the two-lane road. His long skinny middle finger flashed out of the window as he roared by.

"Moron," I said.

My dad clapped me on the shoulder. "Nice work. If there's any justice in the world, there'll be a cop waiting ahead to nail the little bastard."

I felt pretty good about myself. I pressed the accelerator and eased the Buick to the speed limit. Dad whistled an old Ernest Tubb song from the passenger seat, more at ease now with me behind the wheel. His hand, which once clenched the armrest for dear life, now hung outside the open window and his fingertips drummed on the side of the car to the beat of the song in his head. I couldn't understand why such a tense incident relaxed him, but it did.

Five blocks later, the flashing red and blue lights of John Q. Lawman parked behind the same beat up Camaro who tried to run us off the road. I half expected my dad to make me pull over so he could tell the cop about the idiot in his custody. As we rolled past, the greasy haired youth smoldered in the front seat. My father surprised me once again by lifting his hand and extending his middle finger at the delinquent, grinning from ear to ear. The kid saw it and could do nothing but grit his teeth. My dad could be pretty cool when he wanted to be.

CHAPTER SEVENTEEN

Diane's eyes flew wide at Renny and company gaining on us. "Oh God, what are we going to do?"

Ideas flashed through my mind such as gunning it and trying to outrun the Mustang. However, I wasn't sure I could control this beast at any high rate of speed. My remaining option was to follow my dear old dad's advice.

Diane's voice climbed several octaves. "What are you doing?"

"Chill out. I'm slowing down. It'll really piss them off."

"Oh, great idea. Instead of trying to get away, we'll piss them off. That way, when they catch us, they'll kill you instead of just putting you in the hospital. Smart thinking, Jack."

My plan worked. The Mustang cruised within a hair's width of my bumper, blaring his horn and flashing his brights. Renny hung out the passenger window and screamed a barrage of obscenities at me, most of which involved my mother and I committing explicit sexual acts which were not only disgusting but physically impossible.

When the white lines of the road grew farther and farther apart, I was at the point where I couldn't go any slower without stopping. Renny hung behind us, and it dawned on me, with some measure of panic, this was far different from the situation a couple of months ago when my dad and I went for my first drive. This was personal, not some stranger who was in a hurry to get somewhere. Renny would follow us wherever we went, now more intent than ever at crushing my skull.

The car lurched forward as the front bumper of the Mustang smacked into the rear of the Buick. I shot a glance to the rearview mirror and focused on Renny's wild face. His primeval scream pierced the night as he howled in triumph. The car lurched forward again as the Mustang took a second shot, hitting us harder this time.

Diane's nails dug into my arm. "Jack, do something."

Slowing down accomplished nothing but giving me whiplash from getting rear ended, so I slammed the gas pedal to the floor and the powerful V-8 roared as we shot forward like a bullet from a gun. My thoughts were of escape, breaking the law be damned. The Mustang dropped back for a moment, the driver caught off guard at my maneuver. The speedometer climbed past sixty as I shot through a light flashing to red as we flew by. The Mustang was trapped at the light, unable to run it before the turning lanes of traffic cut him off. I blew out the tension from my lungs and let off the accelerator, watching the speedometer drop. My eyes snapped to the rearview mirror when the siren blared behind me.

I pulled over into a nearby parking lot as the cop stopped behind me. Back at the intersection, the Mustang darted forward and turned onto the highway, unwilling to risk the chance of me fingering him for the crime. As it faded into the night, a blinding flash of light greeted me.

"In a hurry there, cowboy?" the cop asked.

Gazing at the stern-faced officer, my predicament

bloomed in the glare of his flashlight. Speeding well beyond the posted limit, I'd ran through a red light and knew the rear end to my father's baby lay in shambles. I couldn't finger Renny because I was clueless about the driver, didn't have a license plate number and couldn't even remember the color the Mustang.

"I'm glad you're here," I said, a cold sweat breaking out on my brow.

The cop wrote on a miniature notepad. "Really, that's a new one. Why don't you tell me whatever story you've managed to concoct? I'm in the mood for a laugh."

My spirits sank as I realized the task before me wasn't going to be easy. Etched on the cop's weathered face were hundreds of tales of proclaimed innocence, and I was sure my song and dance, though the absolute truth, would be no different. The cop's face morphed into the enraged face of my father. Regardless of the outcome, or if Renny and his cohorts were caught, it would be a long time before I climbed behind the wheel of Dad's Buick again.

I spent the summer behind a mammoth stainless steel sink, hiding behind mountainous piles of food-encrusted dinnerware in the dish room at the Bronze Café. Mike toiled behind me, unloading the dishes from the Hobart and running them to the kitchen where sweaty, underpaid cooks slopped food and tossed plates to the waitresses who barked out orders. With every drop of sweat rolling across the frowning crevices in my face, I thought of the money I owed my father for the new bumper on the Buick.

Dad showed surprising calm considering I bashed in the rear of his car on the first night I had my license. Once he overcame his initial disbelief, he listened to my story, nodding and grunting as I related the affair in excruciating detail. I showed him the ticket the cop gave me for running the red light and told him of the officer's promise to be on the lookout for the Mustang. He took it in, like a judge in a murder trial. Replacing the flowing black robe was one of powder blue terry cloth, and his gavel was the remote control for the television. I finished my story and waited in agonizing silence for his ruling which would sentence me to death by hanging or life imprisonment in my room with no chance for parole. I'd given up any hope of an acquittal.

"Is that it?" he asked at last.

"Yes, sir," I replied.

His brown eyes narrowed as he opened his mouth to speak before closing it again, the nostrils from his flattened nose flaring. My mother chewed her bottom lip in the visitor's section of the courtroom, wringing her hands while awaiting the verdict. Her hands clutched the pillow in front of her, the pleading eyes of a concerned mother cast toward my father. Diane white-knuckled her purse, eyes wide like a pleading, lost puppy to the judge. She too had a vested interest in the outcome of these proceedings.

"Diane," my father said, "do you want to add anything?"

I slid my eyes to Diane, bewildered at the judge's strategic move. If Diane faltered, if she stuttered, hesitated or showed any sign of balking at my story, I would be sentenced to the gas chamber, never to be heard from again. My dad knew this. The old man was the keenest judge of lying I'd ever seen or would ever hope to. He smelled dishonesty like a dog smells fear. I was frankly surprised he hadn't segregated us and questioned us separately.

Diane locked her eyes on my father's. "No, Mr. Phipps, it happened exactly like Jack said. It wasn't his fault."

Dad turned his contemplation back on me, stumped by what he should do. I thought he might recess the court and delay his ruling until the morning.

"Well, son, by your account the entire accident wasn't your fault, correct?"

"Correct," I said.

"You did nothing to provoke this Renny or his friend?"

"Nothing, Dad. Why would I provoke a psychopath? He just hates me. One minute we're cruising Metcalf, the next he screamed up behind us and rammed your car."

He sucked in and exaggerated breath and blew it out. "Okay, I believe you."

I wanted to leap for joy and weep like an accused criminal pronounced innocent of crimes he didn't commit. The people in the courtroom would have cheered, and the judge would have to bang his gavel against his throne to get them to quiet, threatening to clear the courtroom. The reporters in the gallery would make a mad dash for the nearest telephone, anxious to call in the news so it could be splashed across the front page of the latest edition. I was vindicated.

"But, you're going to pay for the bumper," he said.

The reporters froze, notepads in hand. The celebratory members of the courtroom locked in mid-hug, incredulous at the judge's last statement. Silence filled the room, and the wallet in my pocket shrank as the ghosts of dollars I had yet to earn floated into the pocket of my father in his recliner.

I leapt to my feet in exasperation. "But, it wasn't my fault. You said so yourself."

"I know I did."

"So, why should I have to pay for it?"

"Why should you pay for it? No, Jack, the question is why should *I* have to pay for it. I wasn't the one driving, you were."

His logic stunned me. After it sunk in for a moment, I realized with great dismay and a fair amount of anger he was right. If I thought long and hard, I would have come to the same conclusion. As unfair and wrong as it seemed, the old man was right.

"I know it's a crappy deal, son," he said. "But one of life's lessons you have to learn is there are no free rides, and sometimes things cost you even if it wasn't your fault. This guy may have rear-ended you, but the fact remains you were behind the wheel of my car when it happened. My insurance will pick up the cost of the bumper and the other damage, but I think you should pay the deductible."

My shoulders slumped in defeat. "Oh, man. How much is that?"

"Three hundred and fifty bucks."

I tried to calculate in my mind how many hours I would have to slave away washing food off someone else's plates to pay for the bumper. I tried to calculate how many lawns I would have to mow and vast quantities of weeds I would be forced to pluck from Mom's garden. It was mind-numbing. I rose from my seated position on the witness stand, grabbed the hand of my soon-to-be-lonely-on-the-weekend's girlfriend and trudged up the stairs to my room.

"At least you're not grounded," Diane said once we were in my room.

"I'm leaping at my good fortune, honey."

"Well," she said, snuggling to me on my bed, her slim, sexy legs pressed against mine. "I bet I could clear away those nasty financial blues."

My hormones cranked into overdrive at the thought of her being so close. When she leaned over and sucked on my earlobe, rubbing her hand on the inside of my knee, I thought I would die. We'd kissed and messed around before, but she hadn't executed such a move of maddening seductiveness. The wetness of her tongue and hot breath on my ear flipped the light switch, and I wanted her more than anything I'd ever wanted before.

The thought of making love to her wasn't a sort of dirty fantasy. At this time-stopping moment, it was closer to a reality than I'd ever considered possible. The danger of the driving incident with Renny flipped her switch. With her lick of the earlobe and the ensuing kiss, I didn't look at Diane in quite the innocent way as before. At that moment, in the summer of 1985, we crossed the invisible line from friends to lovers even though we had yet to consummate the deal.

CHAPTER EIGHTEEN

Finding the parties during high school was something of an art and an introduction into the adult world of politics. It was a matter of who you knew and the green you could slap in somebody's palm to get them to divulge the secret locations of the best beer-soaked weekend bashes. When Mike schmoozed the information out of those who held it, it was like poetry in motion. In a world of handshakes and smiles, my best friend Mike was such a natural I knew he'd be running this great nation of ours by the time he hit forty. If there would've been babies around, Mike would kiss them.

Our high school could be pretty cliquish when it wanted to be, depending on the time of the year. During football and basketball season, the jocks stuck with the jocks. During track and baseball, those fall sport players who didn't make the baseball team would hang around with anyone who would hand them a cold beer. The druggies hung out in the smoking lounge on the west side of the school, huddled in masses, bumming Marlboros and matches. During the warm weather, the jocks would go outside and fraternize with the smokers who hung out at the edge of the smoking lounge closest to the stairs, but for the most part kept with their own kind.

During my sophomore year, I felt more comfortable with the jocks. Now, as a junior, I was caught somewhere in between of the jocks and the druggies. I had my friends on both sides, tending to lean more toward the jocks since I played football, but I couldn't reach the level of dedication where I lived for sports, parties and trying to nail any girl in a skirt with a pair of breasts and a pulse. Diane fell much into the same boat. We were both seventeen and a couple since the age of eight representing a longer timespan than most of our friends' parents could stand each other.

There was one serious challenger to Diane's throne in high school—a smoking hot soccer player named Amy Milardo with sculpted bronze legs stretching to the heavens. To be honest, I was very attracted to her, and if Diane weren't around, we would have hooked up in a heartbeat. Amy chased after me for several months, her bright teeth always flashing my way like a supernova when Diane lingered near. If Diane were a cat, her back hairs would have bristled and her ears lay back at Amy's approach. One of the gnarliest fights of our relationship came from a theoretical discussion about whether or not I would go out with Amy if Diane and I weren't together. I made the colossal mistake of playing the "what if" game by saying "probably." It took a month to melt the iceberg Diane put between us.

When Amy started going hard and heavy with Johnny Bay, the imminent threat ended and we returned to normal. People went back to assuming we would be married by the time we finished high school. I mean, we were Jack and Diane, the Inseparables. Nobody we knew heard the famous John Cougar ballad without conjuring an image of the two of us. Though we both had our own friends, we didn't belong to a group who always hung out together, lounging at the lake during the summer or huddled by the bonfire at a Tonya Robbs party when her parents would go out of town every other weekend. If more than the two of us, it would be Mike and whatever girl he dated at the time, or Diane's friend Vicki Hauser. It was a random group, and we couldn't quite penetrate the loop of the high school socialites. But, we didn't need to. We had Mike.

"Check it out," Mike said, a smile pasted on his face so wide the corners of his mouth almost touched his ears. "Bobby Tuscari's parents are leaving in a mere four hours for a five-day trip to Orlando, and Bobby somehow conned them into letting him stay."

"No way," I said, exchanging high fives at the exciting news. Going to a Bobby Tuscari party was akin to scoring fifty-yard-line tickets to the Super Bowl, except there would be less violence at the football game. Keeping it quiet must have been a calculated move on Bobby's part. It was Friday afternoon and we just caught wind of it. By the time the final bell rang in two hours, it would spread through the school like a pandemic virus. Word of a Bobby Tuscari party burned the gossip grapevine faster than a pile of straw doused in kerosene.

In his young life, Bobby hosted two parties, both of legendary status. Both parties ended with police, broken teeth, and teenagers swarming the streets, vomiting as they went from over-indulging in the abundance of available beer. If you skipped a Tuscari bash, you were doomed to only hear of the astonishing feats of juvenile delinquency and condemned to kicking yourself for missing them.

"When is it?" I asked. "Tonight or tomorrow night?"

"Tonight, after the football game."

"Jesus, I hope he doesn't get hurt in the game."

"Well, guess you guys will have to beat those Raiders so bad they won't be able to lay a finger on our precious quarterback."

I gave Mike another high five, pleased at the prospect of a good party. We couldn't remember the last time someone threw a good bash, and we formulated a plan of action. Since I played in the game, and Diane would be leading the cheer squad on the sidelines, Mike would hang with Vicki in the stands. After the game while the coach patted us on the back or chewed our asses out depending on the score, I would shower and meet them at the party.

"You bringing Angela?" I asked.

"Nah," he said. "That wasn't going anywhere. I dumped her."

"What's the matter, Mikey? She didn't put out on the first date?"

He punched me in the shoulder. "Up yours, Phipps. Besides, it was the second date."

"You're a slut, Washington."

We hopped from the bench in the commons area, hoisting my backpack over my shoulder and trudging toward Biology. Mike had Algebra two doors down.

"I'll be hanging out with your wife at the party until you get there."

"Yeah," I said, used to him calling Diane my wife. "Just don't get any ideas on keeping her warm."

Mike laughed. "She wishes. See you in a few."

We parted ways and I cruised to the back of the room, took a seat and watched Mr. Zipp draw anatomical shapes on the chalkboard. I opened my playbook, studying the defenses we would run in tonight's game and the offensive sets to be thrown our way. My thoughts drifted far from football and anatomy to imagined things which could happen tonight. A palpable vibe of excitement hung in the air, indicating something special would happen tonight, something we would relive long after we left these hallowed halls. I wouldn't miss it for the world.

CHAPTER NINETEEN

The football game must have been exciting and fun for the fans in the stands, but it sucked for those of us on the turf. We hunkered on the field, bloodied and bruised beyond comprehension, wondering what in the hell happened over four quarters. We were the better team—bigger, stronger, faster, and expected to dominate. Yet here we were, our backs against the goal line, somehow losing to the 2-6 Raiders by the score of 13-7 with less than two minutes to go.

We gathered in the huddle during our final timeout, tight-lipped, alternating our bloodshot eyes between the frozen clock and the football resting on the one-yard line. Second and goal with mere inches separating the Raiders from sealing the victory with the proverbial dagger through the heart.

I tried to catch a glimpse of Diane on the sidelines for inspiration, but I couldn't spot her over the glare of the Friday night lights. Exhaustion tugged at my frame, every cell in my body devoid of energy. It was the most brutal, physical game I ever encountered, and through the course of the battle, I kept wondering how these guys were 2-6. Tonight, against the best team in the league, they played as if this were the Super Bowl.

We slapped each other on the helmets, revving ourselves up. I took my position on the corner of the defense, eyeballing the lanky wide receiver who'd tested me all night. So far, he'd made three catches for forty yards, well below his average so I was doing well. Across the line, fire burned in his dark eyes. He wasn't finished yet.

The teams took their spots, the muddied and bloodied hands of the lineman dug into the ripped-up turf, breath steaming into the cold night air like bulls readying to charge the matador. When the quarterback crouched under center, he slipped a prolonged glance to the receiver in front of me, a dead giveaway the ball headed this way. A hoard of butterflies released in my stomach, the urge to vomit lurking in the background.

After a few signal calls and a bark from the quarterback, the center snapped the ball. The receiver came straight at me, arms held close to his body with his gloved palms up. It was a running play to my side. I started forward, spotting the quarterback pitching the ball to his right into the waiting arms of Number 24, a bruising running back with thighs as thick as tree trunks and the speed of a cheetah. He would later go on to play at the University of Nebraska. He was that good.

When the receiver and I met, I pulled a swim move on him and pushed him to the side, giving me a clear shot at the oncoming freight train. As the distance between us closed, the whites of his eyes flashed and his nostrils flared. He steamrolled to his right, angling toward the sideline, trying to beat me outside. I sprinted forward, legs burning, lungs aching with my eyes glued to his hips and the ball swinging back and forth like a pendulum in his thick arms.

I ran in slow motion, the crowd falling silent, leaving just the grunts of players and the crack of helmets meeting behind me. It was one on one, just me and Number 24. If I missed the tackle, they won and our playoff dreams would be shattered. If I made it, we would live to fight another down.

As we drew closer, I realized he was running out of real estate, the sideline looming near. As he cut it back, I sprung forward with the miniscule amount of energy left in my tired legs. With an epic crack of pads we collided, my helmet striking the end of the football, and my shoulder smacking into his barrel chest, like running full speed into a brick wall. I blacked out for a moment.

When the darkness dissipated, I spotted Number 24 lying flat on his back three feet away, surveilling the sky with glassy eyes. The yard marker lay ten feet from us. He hadn't scored and sprawled on the ground empty handed. As the crowd roared, I rolled onto my stomach, painful claws ripping at my shoulder. Sixty yards downfield, our safety ran unopposed the opposite way with the ball held high over his head.

A few of my teammates came back to help me up, screaming in my face and grabbing my facemask. The world still wavered a bit, but my adrenaline surged at the view of Number 24 still lying on the field with a couple of trainers around him. I slogged to the sidelines, and my own team assaulted me, smacking my helmet so hard my ears rang worse than they already were.

"Phipps," Coach yelled, grabbing my face mask and yanking me close. "That was the hardest goddamn hit I've seen in my life. Good work, son."

We went on to kick the extra point and win the game. Looking back, the most exciting thing for me wasn't our victory because of the fumble I'd caused or going to the playoffs. It was seeing Number 24 on the bench, wearing the same expression

I imagined he'd wear if he got smashed in the face with a sledgehammer. It was knowing my number was tattooed on his chest.

CHAPTER TWENTY

I was the man of the hour entering the Tuscari household. Word spread to those who didn't attend the game that I caused the game-winning fumble, and the party goers assaulted me as I made my way through the house on the prowl for Diane. Some of the pounding I took at the party was worse than any hit I'd taken during the game, like being run through the drunken gauntlet. I was the king on the throne, and if I would have known how brief my reign would be, I would have relished it more.

Diane caught a ride with Mike instead of waiting for me after the game since the post-game wrap-up was always a long, drawn-out process. The man code required Coach to talk far longer than he should, wowing us with how well we played, but where we could have done better. Conversely, if we lost, he wowed us with how crappy we played and where we could have done better. Either way, we had to suffer through the drudgery of our misdoings.

I found Mike by the keg, putting the moves on a pretty girl I'd noticed wandering around the hallowed halls of our school. I couldn't tell from her expression what her level of interest was in my best friend, but he would give it his all. I couldn't find Diane anywhere, though everyone I asked just saw her a minute ago.

I wriggled my way through the crowd toward the living room. A group of wrestlers engaged in a raging game of Quarters on the Tuscari's glass dining room table which would inevitably end up shattered by the end of the night. The music blared at such a volume the identity of the artist was unintelligible. Combine the volume of the tunes with the whoops of drunken revelers and shouted fragments of conversation, and it was impossible to hear myself think.

Acrid cigarette smoke doused the air, and my feet stuck to the floor from spilled beer and wine coolers. The collective crowd was three sheets to the wind, the telltale sign of a Tuscari party. Nobody left sober and I estimated at least fifty percent of the population would be blowing chunks within hours. Hal Mooreland was passed out, sprawled across the kitchen counter with messages scrawled in magic marker on his naked torso. Jeanie Rind spun alone by the sink to some tune that didn't match the Guns and Roses blaring from the stereo. Jimmy Quinton and Barb Penny tongue wrestled in the hallway leading to the bedrooms, while three nearby guys exchanged cash bets on how long it would take them to get naked.

I reached the living room and stopped to take in the awesome spectacle of my fellow students crammed in like sardines. Anyone suffering from claustrophobia would collapse from a brain seizure at the mere sight of the crowd. Their body, unable to fall to the ground, would be supported by the sweaty, screaming bodies of their fellow partiers.

With the masses jammed in the room, I was amazed I managed to catch a glimpse of Diane on the couch. She wasn't alone. It wasn't Mike, Angela or anybody else from our usual crew at her side. Snuggled too close to the woman I loved, the woman whom I'd been with for as long as I could remember, was an absolute hunk of a lad. I mean, I'm not a homosexual, but if I was, I would have given consideration to this guy. For the first time in my life, the flicker of the jealously flame lit with an audible scratch of the match on the book. An immediate deposit of acid dropped in my stomach, the burning sensation of the green monster.

The closer I got, the higher the green flame grew as I observed the way Diane reacted to him. They faced each other on the couch, his dark eyes boring into hers, his pearl-white teeth flashing such brightness I'm surprised she didn't have to wear sunglasses. His face was chiseled from a formed slab of granite under model perfect hair along with impeccable clothes that made him look like he just stepped from a modeling catalog. He wasn't from our school, because I would have heard the chattering banter of giggling girls talking about him.

Diane's beautiful face glowed with laughter. Her long legs drew underneath her as she lounged sideways on the couch, leaning into the conversation. Her left elbow crooked on the top of the couch, the hand holding a half full plastic red cup of beer. Her right hand rested on her knee, scant inches from his. The smile I'd forgotten adorned her face, and I couldn't remember the last time she looked at me in that manner.

I thought my imagination blew things up worse than they were. She wasn't interested in this guy. It was somebody's cousin visiting from out of town or one of her friend's boyfriends she kept company until they got back from the keg. We'd been together so long and been through so much she couldn't want anything to do with this guy. I loved her more than anything in the world, and she felt the same way about me. That's how it had always been. We were soul mates, destined to be together until the end of the earth.

That's what I thought as I reached the couch and stood above them. There was nothing to fear. But, when He-Man noticed me above them and Diane followed suit, a chink formed in our impervious armor. She blushed like a kid caught with her hand in the cookie jar, guilt sagging her features like wet bags of sand.

"Hi," I said, an edge on my voice. I couldn't tell if I was depressed or angry. However I sounded, I think they both sensed the negative tone.

Diane jumped to her feet. "Oh….hi, Jack." She made no move to hug or kiss me, stuck in the Never Never Land of Awkwardness. She shot a glance to He-Man who pressed to his feet.

He had a good three inches of height on me with a thick chest and veins popping from his biceps. As we glared at each other, I hoped for the embarrassed darting of his eyes, the signal he knew he was sniffing around another dog's turf, but his sky-blue eyes laser locked on me. He'd been told this lady was off-the-market and didn't care. He would pounce without a second thought as long as it was in his best interest. This guy was a user and a taker.

"Jack," Diane said. "This is Zack Hunter. He goes to South. Zack…this is Jack."

She may as well have shot an arrow through my heart and poured salt in the open wound. In any social setting, she introduced me with great pleasure as her boyfriend Jack. To hear my name coming from her mouth without the boyfriend appendage was the worst thing anyone ever said to me.

"Great game," she said, breaking the silence. "Everyone's talking about it."

"Yeah," Zack the He-Man said, the right side of his mouth rising into a smirk, "word is you guys got lucky at the end."

My eyes hardened and narrowed, hands tingling as the floodgates of adrenaline opened wide. The snarky comment was a shot across the bow, a probing jab to see how I'd react. Diane's eyes darted back and forth between us as she rocked from one leg to another, unsure which way to go.

"I don't think luck had anything to do with it, Zed," I said.

"Zack."

"Whatever," I said, my heart thundering.

The conversation around us quieted, and I was certain someone lowered the stereo volume a notch or two. The crowd around us sucked in tight from the tension in the air and the scent of impending bloodshed. After all, this was a Tuscari party, and there's always a fight at a Tuscari party. I didn't think I'd be the one throwing the punches.

Diane waited in silence like a slug, unable to make a move in either direction. It dawned on me this wasn't the first time these two met. He-Man wouldn't lather on the testosterone if he'd just met her. After all, she couldn't have beat me to the party by more than a half hour.

"Is there a problem?" Zack asked, taking a half step toward me. His jaw clenched and pulsated, and I noticed a faint, but lengthy scar crossing his upper lip. I wondered where he'd gotten it.

"I don't know, you tell me."

Diane put her hand on my elbow. "Don't be like this. We were just talking."

"Yeah, Jack. Don't worry, we didn't have time to do anything else… yet. Why don't you go grab a glass of milk and give us some more time?"

I don't think I've ever moved as fast and as furious as I did in that moment. My fist balled and flew at the speed of sound toward his stone jaw. When it connected, pain shot through my arm, and He-Man crashed to the couch. I pounced on top of him ignoring Diane's screams.

I wasn't much of a fighter. I'd been in a few shoving scuffles through the years, but the only punches I'd thrown were aimed at Jimmy Galdano in grade school. Now, my fists flew on their own accord, striking bone and ripping flesh. I would like to say I pummeled this guy out of existence, but it would be a lie. I would even like to say I won the fight, but that too would be a lie. He was stronger and more experienced than I. He took his fair share of punishment, but in the end, it was me lying on the cold, wet grass in the Tuscari front yard. I didn't even remember how we landed there.

Through an already swollen eye, the copper tinge of blood on my lips, Zack Hunter towered above me. I'd ripped his shirt, bloodied his nose and there was a hell of a lump forming below his right eye, but he wore the shit-eating grin of victory. I'd gotten him good, but he was the one standing, restrained by several of my teammates. Diane stood in shocked horror, tears streaking her beautiful Judas face. Mike grabbed my elbow and helped me to my feet. The earth wavered beneath my feet, but I held my ground, wondering what happened. Zack yelled something at me, but his words couldn't penetrate the ringing in my ears. Diane took a couple of steps toward me, but stopped.

There were tears in her eyes, her mouth trembling, trying to hold back whatever emotions whirled in her head. It broke my heart to see her like that, like she wanted to tear herself in two pieces and be able to go both ways. She was sorry, but it didn't matter to me. The image of her on the couch with the smile once reserved for me was forever stamped on my brain.

"Why?" I asked her at last. Without waiting for an answer, I limped down the car-lined street, Mike helping me stay on my feet. Neither of us said a word on the way to my car. We passed people running toward the Tuscari bash, gasping as they passed what was left of me. I must have been quite the spectacle.

Diane didn't chase after me trying to explain what happened. She let me go. That was what bothered me most about the entire ordeal—she let me go. As my feet plodded and scraped their way down the wet asphalt, what hurt even more was that part of me let her go too.

CHAPTER TWENTY-ONE

When you're seventeen, you think you know it all. It comes down to the fact that anyone old enough to be your parents who disagrees with you has been over-the-hill for so long they've forgotten what it's like to have such an incredible knowledge base. This theory, of course, is so riddled full of holes it looks like Swiss cheese. But, in my thought process at the time, the holes existed in the non-important sectors of life like how the Korean War started or how to develop a spending budget, things people like only your parents knew or cared about. My dad knew more than I would ever hope to know, but was the last one I'd turn to when it came to matters of the heart. My brother held as much knowledge of love as a turnip, and Mom would slobber over me, wondering how I'd gotten in such a condition and want to take me to the emergency room for a full-body scan.

For these reasons, I didn't go into the house when I arrived home. It was a hair before midnight, and from the flickers of light through the closed curtains, I surmised my father slept in his chair, watching some black and white war movie through closed eyelids. I would need to wait at least another half hour until my mother realized he fell asleep downstairs and came to fetch him to bed. Jake painted the town red with his buddies, cruising until his one o'clock curfew, drinking beer, cranking the tunes, and searching for a woman to give her virtue to him.

I sat in the driveway in my mom's car, the engine clicking as it cooled, the radio silent for the first time in years, the weight of the world pressing me into a compact ball of anger and despair. I probed the cuts and bruises on my face, body aching and head pounding when an overwhelming sense of loneliness descended upon me. All I ever knew was Diane Riven. Though I hadn't given a concerted thought to my future, I'd assumed it would include her. I hadn't lost her yet, but the ornate tapestry I'd woven in my mind depicting love now lay in ragged tatters at my feet. I wished she didn't live so close to me.

If we broke up, it would be complete and utter torture. I would be able to stalk her from my bedroom window and spot her across the street. She would talk on the phone, facing the window without noticing me. The cars would pull in front of her house, and young suitors would bounce up the walk in great jubilation. Mr. Riven would fling open the front door and welcome them with open arms, thankful they were anyone but the worthless Phipps kid from across the street.

Hot tears rolled as I realized how much this would hurt. The unthinkable end of us hadn't happened yet, but it seemed inevitable. On the drive home, I tried to convince myself I imagined the whole thing and over-reacted. The harder I tried, the more I reflected on the last year. The more I reflected, the more I realized things weren't right between us for months, but I cast a blind eye to it. Our passion cooled and making out was a mere afterthought when nothing else aired on TV and my parents were asleep. But, the key for me was the smile she gave the other guy that used to be reserved for me. The thought of her beautiful face opened the floodgates, and I leaned my head on the steering wheel sobbing.

Minutes later, the sobbing stopped, but I couldn't lift my head from the wheel. A squeal of brakes and a rattling muffler announced the arrival of Mike's car. Diane's voice said something, and my best friend's car turned into its own driveway. I froze in place, terrified at raising my head to see Diane, yet desperately wanting to do so. It wasn't until she knocked on my passenger window that I mustered the courage to look her in the eye. She waited for an invite, her arrival both welcome and painful. I waved her in.

"Hi," she said, her voice a whisper as she settled into the passenger seat. I focused my attention to the garage door in front of me.

"Hey," I said.

"You okay?"

"Not really."

"Me either," she said. "Do you want to talk?"

"What's to talk about?" The truth was I didn't know if I wanted to discuss the events at the party.

"Nothing happened, Jack. He's just a friend."

I bore through her face with my narrowed eyes. Her lie unleashed the anger coiling and compressing within me for the last hour.

My tone was as sharp as a blade. "Bullshit, Diane. Do you think I'm a moron?"

She flinched at the harshness of my tone, and I sucked in air to try to slow my racing pulse.

"Do you think I'm a moron?" I repeated, softer but still edgy.

"No, I don't."

"Then why are you treating me like one? You think I couldn't see the way you looked at him? You think I'm blind? Do you think after all this time together I don't know you?"

"I'm sorry." Tears welled in her eyes and the effect took the edge off my anger.

"I'm sorry too. I have to know why."

"I can't answer that." A tear dripped from her cheek onto her jacket.

"Can't or won't?"

"Can't. I don't know why I acted the way I did toward him. Maybe it was the way he looked at me. Maybe it was the way I could tell he wanted me, the way you wanted Amy Milardo. I know you love me, but I haven't gotten that vibe from you in such a long time."

I wanted to lie and tell her it wasn't true. I wanted to throw the line back in her face as a bunch of Cosmopolitan garbage, but I couldn't. I hadn't lied to her before, and I wasn't going to start now.

"I know," I said. "What happened to us? It's like we're our parents anymore. Hanging out together more like friends than lovers. Jesus, we're too young to feel like this."

"I know. Nobody believes we've been together this long and haven't slept together yet."

"There's more to us than sex, Diane," I said, offended she brought up our virgin status, an idea much more hers than mine.

"But that's it. We haven't had sex yet. We haven't even fooled around hot and heavy for months now. And it's not because I don't love you or want to be with you because I do. It's like somebody poured water on the fire."

"And He-Man lit your flame," I said.

"In a way, yes. He's a jerk, Jack. I don't want him. But I want what he sees in me. I want to be desirable, I want you to want me. We've treated each other like buddies for such a long time, and it has to change if we're going to get anywhere. And I want us to get somewhere."

"Do you mean it?"

"With all I've got. I love you."

"I love you too, Diane."

She crossed the seat and held me close, kissing away the pain from the bruises, kissing away the aches from the cuts, healing the gaping wound in my heart and lifting the world off my shoulders. Lost in her eyes again, the world swam back into focus.

I took her by the hand and led her into my house, creeping to the basement. We entered the extra bedroom, and I locked the door behind us, fumbling at each other under the light of the moon shining through the daylight window. As we undressed, my passion for her filled my soul once again. As we lay on the bed and pressed our naked bodies together for the first time, I was lost in the wonderment of the moment. We made love for the first time that night. It was awkward and scary, but my sheer love for her came out in the darkness. Our love for each other enveloped us and held us in its gentle hands. The pain disappeared, our tears dried and it was once again the two of us.

CHAPTER TWENTY-TWO

We were crammed like sardines in the hot gym, nearly five hundred seniors ready to pounce upon the world. Our vinyl black robes trapped the heat, and we smoldered waiting for the faculty to take the stage so we could grab our diplomas, toss our hats in the air and head for the party. I managed to find my folks in the bleacher crowd, my dad squirming in his seat as he tried to clear some elbow room. I'm sure my mother scolded him to sit still like he was six years old.

Spirits soared among the graduating class of 1987. Reagan controlled Washington, Motley Crue would hit Kansas City next week for a concert, and three glorious months' worth of partying lay ahead of us before we went to college. What else did we need? We were free, liberated from the mandated educational prison to which we served an eighteen-year sentence. All that remained was a walk across the stage, a handshake from Principal Stone, a flip of the tassel and we were history.

Back a few rows, Diane squirmed in her seat, ready to get out of town and hit the college scene. She winked and blew me a kiss. I held up my right hand, crossing my fingers and she did the same.

It was a good year for us. The Zack Hunter incident

faded in the past, and we were once again Jack and Diane, couple extraordinaire. We still had the occasional spat, but overall our relationship was stronger than ever. Once we broke the barrier, we had sex like they would outlaw it in the near future, and I spent a small fortune on condoms. I rotated drug stores so I wouldn't raise any eyebrows with the local checkout ladies. Mike called us the Rabbits, which Diane didn't find amusing.

As we overheated in a black sea of rental robes, growing more impatient by the minute, a chord of sadness struck me. We had less than three months together before hitting our respective college campuses. Diane made the choice to go to the University of Kansas while I would go to Kansas State University—two schools with similar names separated by a hundred miles and different cultures. KU was more upscale in their student body, attracting the rich kids and the dopers who followed the local band scene. K-State was founded as an agricultural school in the late 1800's and attracted the kids from the surrounding rural communities. She would study education while I headed for engineering, specific discipline undecided. We'd already worked out our visitation schedules during the weekends.

It would be strange to spend the majority of my waking moments without Diane. I'd spend the occasional weekend night with the boys, but it was typically the two of us and an entourage of friends and their dates. College would be the longest I'd go without seeing her since my summers on Uncle Will and Aunt Kate's Nebraska farm when I was ten years old. Since we would be roommates at K-State, Mike promised he'd keep me out of trouble, and Angela Simms promised the same of Diane. Neither of us worried about our relationship surviving the distance and time. How naïve we were.

After the caps were tossed, hugs doled out and palms aching from vicious high fives from my fellow high school graduates, Diane and I walked hand in hand to front doors of the school. Our folks wanted to get one last picture of us before we headed out for the night.

My mother showered me with kisses and strangled me with the ferocity of her hug. "I'm so proud of you, Jack,"

"Me too, buddy," my dad said. Behind him, Jake tugged at the coat and tie my father made him wear and rolled his eyes at the sloppy sentiments. "Now, my boy, you ready for your graduation gift?"

I'd given a minor amount of thought about what they might get for me for graduation. I leaned toward a wad of cash hidden inside a sentimental Hallmark greeting card. Instead of reaching into his coat and pulling out an envelope, my father wrapped his arm around my shoulder and led me to the parking lot. Perhaps the gift was in the car.

Our Buick was parked under a light pole in the northwest corner of the lot. Dad told a story about his graduation and the ensuing party in a cornfield afterward. As I wondered what lay in the trunk of the Buick for me, he marched past it to an ebony beauty in the shape of a 1967 Ford Mustang—black leather interior, three-speed, 289 horse engine, monster hood scoop and glass packs on the back end. My dad grinned like the Cheshire Cat from Alice in Wonderland as he reached into his suit coat and pulled out a set of keys.

"No," I said, stopping dead in my tracks. A car? He actually bought me a car?

He tossed the keys in the air. "If you think I'm driving two hours each way to Manhattan because you ran out of laundry, think again. Happy graduation, son."

I was speechless. If I could have done a cartwheel, I would have cracked off a dozen across the jagged, potholed macadam of our parking lot. My wildest dreams didn't involve me holding the keys to such a beauty. I leapt at my dad and squeezed the life from him. I pulled back and stared into his watering eyes.

"I don't know what to say, Pop," I said at last.

"Just tell me you'll do me proud in college."

"I will," I said. We admired the beautiful Mustang a moment longer before I climbed inside. The engine roared to life, a deep and throaty rumble—a lion ready to pounce.

"Remember," he said, "you get a ticket, you're paying."

Hours later, the bonfire crackled, and the beer flowed on the open land of the Thomas family estate. Suzie's family offered their services for the last bash, and I estimated well over half of the class showed up. Howls of joy erupted over the blaring music, and people moved around the bonfire like natives in a primitive dance ritual. Diane and I hung back, watching our friends making idiots out of themselves and laughing until stitches stabbed our sides.

Mike and some junior who'd crashed the party lip locked around the side of the house, Mike trying to convince her to head out to the field for some further exploration. I wondered if there was any room out there for them. Writhing bodies of graduates in heat scattered around the field like land mines. Popular guys coupled with unpopular girls and vice versa. I guess the ceremony of freedom we went through somehow snapped the class barriers, and we were free to procreate with the person of our choice. Of course, the liberal amounts of alcohol flowing at the party didn't help the decision making.

Suzie's dad played gatekeeper from a metal folding chair by the front door of the house, turning away people trying to sneak in. Some wanted to use the bathroom and others the bedroom. To the bathroom seekers, he pointed to the tree line to the left. To the bedroom seekers, he shook his head, pointed to the field on the rights and shouted a recommendation for birth control.

Coach Utt patrolled the front gate, appointing himself the director of traffic for incoming vehicles and the sobriety police for those trying to exit. He snatched away more than a few sets of keys. I wondered what contingency plans were in place for the late morning hours when the plastered teens tried to leave.

Diane slipped her arm around my waist and gave me a tight squeeze and a kiss on the nape of my neck.

"I love you, you know," she said.

I faced her and pulled her close. "I do know. Can you believe it's over?"

"No, I can't. It doesn't seem real yet."

"I don't think it will until we hit campus."

She lowered her eyes, finding something of great interest on my shirt. Her weight increased in my arms.

"Are you worried, Jack?"

"About what?"

"Us."

"Because we're going to separate schools?"

"Yeah. I mean, they're not that far apart," she said, plucking at a button on my shirt, "but it's going to be hard. I'm going to miss you."

"I'll miss you too, honey." I pulled her closer, and stroked her back and hair. "I was thinking about it before the graduation ceremony."

"Are you? Worried, I mean."

"I think it will be good for us," I said. "I mean, it'll suck and our phone bills will be outrageous, but we'll be that much stronger when it's over."

"I get worried you'll find someone else," she said, whispering her fear. "Somebody will be there for you more than I can. I know these summer months are going to go by so fast and then we'll be apart."

"You could go to K-State. They have a great education department." I didn't know if it was true, but I hoped my lie sounded authentic.

"KU has a great engineering school, too. We've been over this before."

I'd given it a lot of thought, but I couldn't picture myself in that culture or on that campus. I toured it, walked the massive hills and drank in the local bars. I was like a stranger in a strange land in Lawrence, even surrounded by a crowd of friends. Manhattan and the K-State campus were more my style. Diane felt the same way about KU so debating the topic was a moot point.

We didn't talk for a while, content to hold each other by the fire while our drunken classmates jumped and screamed around us. We were trapped by conflicting desires, both wanting to jump into the future with both feet, but clinging onto the past where our relationship was solid and firm. We claimed everything would be fine, we would make it through the next four to five years, but the truth of the matter was we both knew we were lying. We hoped we would stay together. We dreamed of making it through that period of change and coming out unscathed on the other side. All of this we hoped, yet we were sitting on the doubt and the fear that this experience would tear us apart. We both worried, but wouldn't discuss it. It was safer to talk in certainties.

As the party raged on, we held each other in a comfortable silence, oblivious to the debauchery around us. Our dreams and our hopes lay ahead of us, not set in stone, but swirling in a misty fog of uncertainty. We knew we would try to hold on, a desperate attempt to bask in the security of our love for each other, but this presented uncharted territory. I loved her more than anything in the world, and it killed me to know the possibility existed she wouldn't be there down the road. I tried to shake these ghosts of pessimism, but they dug their claws deep. As my mother said, if it was meant to be, it was meant to be. I guess we would have to wait and see.

CHAPTER TWENTY-THREE

Mike and I were culinary wonders on our final day as line cooks at the Bronze Cafe. Over the years, we'd moved from dishwashers, to bus boys, to prep cooks and then to the highest non-management position available for a couple of high school kids. We grilled the steaks, made the burritos, created wondrous enchiladas and dirty rice spicy enough to bring tears to your eyes. We were almost sorry to leave the joint.

"Hey, Wonder Twins," Eduardo shouted. Eduardo was the owner of the Bronze Café. He'd turned over the management of the place to his nephew, a hopeless little twit with a quarter of a brain and rotted teeth. Eduardo stopped by on occasion to make sure the place was up and running. He'd worn his doubts on his sleeve when Fat Man made us both cooks, but we proved we could do the job. He'd named us the Wonder Twins from the old Superfriends cartoon despite our fervent objections.

I rolled a burrito. "Hey Eduardo, we're making you lots of money tonight."

"That's what I like to hear, amigo. I'll be back in the office when you're done."

Mike slopped rice onto a plate and threw it up in the service window. "What are you doing after work?"

"Diane and I are having our last date before she leaves for KU."

"You packed up?"

"I guess," I said, throwing a couple of specials on the counter above and ringing the bell for one of the waitresses.

"You don't sound too excited."

"I guess you could say my enthusiasm has waned now that it's here."

Mike stopped stirring caked-on enchilada sauce from a pan and glared at me. I continued forming another burrito. We had this conversation a month ago while in my room playing Tecmo Bowl on my Nintendo. I moped about being away from Diane, and he pointed out how much fun he and I would have. The pros and cons of each situation swayed on the scales in my head, the con side winning out despite the continual poundage Mike added to the pro side.

"Man, are you going to do this for the next four years?"

"Do what?" I asked, knowing what was coming and in no mood to hear it.

Mike tossed the pan to the side and walked to me. "Look, man. You and Diane are going to be fine. I know that, she knows that and pretty much the rest of the free world knows that. The only person on this planet who doesn't know is you."

He stalked back across the kitchen to let me stew in his profound insightfulness. As usual, Mike was right. It wasn't a surprise when he became a psychologist. I patted him on the back as I walked past him to tend the grill.

My problem then, and one which still plagues me to some degree, is I suffer from an overactive imagination. I suppose that's why I write. But while the imagination is often a wonderful tool, its sometimes a hazardous thing. It puts your weird subconscious thoughts into play, spinning the reels of some whacked-out movie machine and putting the unconscious on the screen of the mind. You can't stop it, you can't change it. Trying to halt some of these fantasies was as futile as trying to flush the image of an elephant from your mind when someone tells you not to think of one.

Over the last several months, my imagination crept up on me, putting stupid and pointless fantasies in my head involving Diane and the entire male population at the University of Kansas. I kept picturing her at bars like the Hawk or the Wheel, beer in hand and some sleezeball guy trying to put the moves on her. She would dismiss him with a coy flick of the wrist and the next guy would step up. I would stand helpless outside the bar, fogging the window and getting my greasy fingerprints on the glass in a sad state as the line behind her continued to grow. One of those guys would be my replacement, and I wouldn't even know until after the fact.

Mike derailed my train of thought. "That's the last ticket of the night. You ready to see Eduardo?"

"Let's go," I said, happy the nightmare vision faded.

Eduardo waited behind the desk, feet propped on a little filing cabinet against the wall. He waved us in and invited us to sit on plastic pickle buckets doubling as stools. He indulged us with praise of our great work for the company. It amused me when he referred to the Bronze Café as the "Company" since it was Eduardo's sole venture. After pumping our heads so big I was afraid neither of us would be able to get through the door, he reached into his desk and pulled out two envelopes. Handing them to us, he said they were for good luck in our new adventure.

"You guys have a hell of an opportunity here," he said as we reached for the envelopes. "Don't screw it up."

Mike and I opened the envelopes, in awe at the stack of bills inside. I thumbed through the stack but didn't count it. My father said to never count monetary gifts in front of the giver. Mike's father must be cut from the same cloth because Mike didn't count his either. I was anxious to do it, don't get me wrong. The bills were twenties and plentiful.

"Wow, Eduardo," I said, surprised I could get anything past my thickened tongue. "I don't know what to say."

"Me neither," Mike said.

"Say thank you, you morons," Eduardo said. "That's for college, for when you get in a bind. Don't piss it away on beer or at some strip club."

Mike slipped his envelope inside his jacket pocket. "Thanks, Eduardo. We really appreciate it."

"Just do me a favor," Eduardo said, leaning forward onto the desk, face stern. "Don't take this shit for granted, school I mean. I don't want to sound like your old man, because I know you've probably gotten this same speech from him a hundred times."

"A hundred and fifty at least," I said cracking a grin before stifling it when Eduardo didn't return it.

"You go have fun. You party and nail those college chicks every chance you get. But never, ever forget why you're there. To get an education. I don't want you back here slopping food for seven dollars an hour anytime in the near future because you couldn't get your heads on straight. I want more for you guys. You've been great employees and I'm glad you've worked for me all these years."

Mike and I shook Eduardo's hand, thanking him again for the bonus. He waved us away, I think a bit sad to see us go. We walked out of the restaurant and counted our bonus once we reached my car.

"Holy crap, Jack," Mike said, eyes wide. "There's like four hundred dollars in here."

I was amazed, yet thankful to have worked for a guy like Eduardo. I figured this was a special allotment of the "Company" funds and something he didn't do for everyone who worked for him.

"What are you going to do with yours?" Mike asked.

"Exactly what he said to do," I said. "Save it for a rainy day."

We hopped in my Mustang and headed for home, leaving the Bronze Café behind us. I had to admit, I was pretty excited. The freedom of the world awaited me in a few hours. I grasped life by the tail, and in possession of a fat wallet and a woman who loved me. I counted myself lucky.

CHAPTER TWENTY-FOUR

Oh, this was going to be fun. I stood at the center of Kansas State University in awe at the surroundings and caught in the history of the aged buildings and the learning taking place here. But, the academics paled in comparison to the copious number of gorgeous women strutting around in shorts and miniskirts. There were blondes, brunettes and redheads in abundance on these hallowed grounds, and it was all I could do to keep my tongue in my mouth and not look like a stupid freshman. Diane flashed to the forefront of my brain along with a stab of guilt, but I just looked, right?

I strolled past Ferrell Library, an ancient structure in which I would spend little time. During my four and a half years at K-State, I remember going in the library a total of five times or a little more than once per year. The building was old, musty and suffered from an abundant lack of technology. You couldn't find a book or an article in that joke of a library if you tried. Many years after I graduated, they invested funds into the building to turn it into a first-rate library. When I attended, however, it was a pitiful excuse for an informational depository.

The football team was as pitiful as the library. The Wildcats were the bottom feeders of the Big 8 conference, so bad they contacted me about playing football for them. However, there wasn't an ounce of desire in my bones to try to tackle 230-pound running backs, or chase six-and-a-half-foot-tall wide receivers with my 175-pound frame. Sports Illustrated even did a major spread on our football woes, calling Kansas State "Futility U".

I headed south toward the student union, following the crowd in hopes they would lead me where I needed to go. Coming from the dorms on the opposite side of campus, I wondered how bad this walk would suck in the dead of winter. Manhattan, the home of Kansas State, was two hours west of Kansas City without much around it. The harsh winter winds howled unabated across the plains and cut you like a knife. For now, I was thankful for the plentiful heat and humidity. I would rather sweat than shiver.

Morale was high among the student body, as it always is before classes begin. I always liked the first day of school. Give me new books, a blank notepad and a well-plotted schedule, and I was on cloud nine. In a matter of weeks, the drudgery of going to classes and doing homework would settle upon us, and we would be eager for Christmas vacation or spring break. But, for now, the jubilant students readied for the sun to settle below the horizon so the party could begin. Many couldn't wait for Father Time to creep along, so they imbibed the second their feet hit the campus. You imagined the sweet symphony of beer tabs being pulled around town.

The student union loomed ahead, and Mike waited for me, salivating at the coeds as they passed him. I could tell by his slackened jaw he enjoyed himself.

"Tongue in, Mr. Washington," I said.

"I would say this is a target rich environment, wouldn't you?"

"Wipe the drool from your chin, my man. Women hate guys who slobber."

"This is going to kick ass," he said as his head darted around following the women as if he watched a bizarre tennis match. "I can't decide which one I want."

"Pick one and get rejected so we can get on with this."

"Can you believe this? Where did they come from?"

I followed his eyes tracking a stunning brunette in shorts three sizes too small. "Beats me. It's like they pulled a page from one of my dreams."

We followed the brunette into the Union cafeteria. When she disappeared around the corner, we headed toward the bookstore to shell out extravagant amounts of green for obscure textbooks weighing like a ship's anchor.

The bookstore choked with kids trying to squeeze through the narrow textbook aisles without knocking them to the floor. Frantic student workers trying to earn an extra buck kept a wary eye out for shoplifters while trying to help people find the right books. I managed to locate the ones on my list, buying used books wherever possible to save a few dollars. These books were somewhat ragged around the edges, but were also pre-highlighted. I thumbed through them to check if the previous owner managed to catch the main points. A moron with an exuberant highlighter would be of no value.

After spending an astounding two hundred dollars and change on books, I found a concrete bench outside the bookstore and waited for Mike. My father would have a coronary over the book sum and demand I produce an itemized list. He worried they sold kegs of beer in the student store, and I'd skip the books and go right for the good stuff. I was lucky Dad and Mom planned this out and saved for years. He didn't want me working forty hours a week and trying to get an education at the same time. I was also lucky my brother wasn't the shiniest apple on the cart and passed on the college route, leaving me the balance of the college fund.

On a concrete bench outside the student union, watching my new world swirl around me, I wondered what Diane was doing. I wondered if she too sat in this marvelous world enjoying it as much as I. Did she ogle the guys as they strode past in shorts and tank tops, showing off bronze pecs and cannonball biceps? A twinge of jealousy jerked through my body as my imagination tried to take off and play a scenario out at the KU student union, but I cut it off at the pass. She could enjoy the looking, the admiration for the way the Good Lord put together the anatomy of the opposite sex. I would do the same and let the guilt wash away like water from a duck's back.

Mike emerged and we bitched about the cost of the books and their effect on our weekend beer funds. As we walked toward the exit, we ran into a couple of acquaintances from high school we missed over the summer. They invited us to an opening bash of the school year at some guy's house they met the night before. We secured the address and promised to make an appearance. Walking into the bright sunlight, I whipped out my Ray Ban knockoffs and drew in an exaggerated breath of newfound freedom.

"Mike? I think I'm gonna like it here."

We worked our way back to the dorm, anxious to drop

the four hundred pounds of books we carried over our backs. There was beer to drink, and we were just the guys to do it.

The first few weeks were a blur. I attended my first college classes, a bit overwhelmed at the amount of reading and homework assigned, but at the same time underwhelmed at the level of difficulty. I didn't have to study much in high school and yet was able to maintain a solid 3.6 grade point average. Looking back, I wonder what I might have accomplished if I'd actually tried.

The college professors and their lack of enthusiasm surprised me, destroying my preconceived notion of impassioned old men and women preaching calculus and physics as if they were hellfire and brimstone preachers on a pulpit. Instead, most of them appeared bored and nonchalant, as if they tired of teaching teenagers the complicated formulae and equations.

I liked my English Composition teacher a great deal. She was a savvy, sarcastic woman in her fifties who brought forth the enthusiasm I'd pictured before entering the University. She insisted we call her Nina. She turned boring stories into masterpieces and graded our papers with bright red ink, commenting both on the good and the bad. She let us write what we wanted to write and didn't punish our grades if she didn't agree with our views.

I don't want to make it sound as if my college life was nothing but academics. Oh sure, that's what I told my folks who called every few days to find out what I learned from the money they shelled out. After I spouted off a few calculus or physics theorems, they stammered in awe on the other end of the phone, amazed at what their boy absorbed. Of course, I wouldn't lay money on the fact I got any of those theorems correct, but it didn't matter. They were lost and it masked my love of Aggieville.

Aggieville, a two-block street teeming with bars and restaurants, was my relief valve for the pressures of college. Each bar sported its own kind of crowd, and I made sure I ventured into every one of them to ensure I'd find the right hangout. There was Brothers, a freshman/sophomore dance club where you could drink like a fish even though you were underage. Kites represented the fraternity and sorority hangout. Upperclassmen frequented Auntie Mae's, a dim, narrow bar in the basement of one of the older brick buildings. It was more of a sit-down, visit with your buddies' bar though it was always packed. Bushwackers was another dance bar, though it sat off the strip and only hit capacity during the laugh nights where they would bring in some comedians.

My favorite, and the hotspot on the Aggieville strip, was Rusty's Last Chance Saloon. The front patio held a dozen or so scarred wooden picnic tables open to the elements—a most excellent place to spend a Friday afternoon in the sun after a hard week of homework and tests. Inside, more well-worn, carved up tables sat on a dusty stone floor. Wondrous smells of hamburgers and barbecue floated throughout the joint. Their french fries were long, greasy and delicious. An eclectic mixture of classes and types from the Greek system to the stoners made up the crowd at the bar. Everyone was a friend at Last Chance, one of the reasons it held my number one slot.

Diane loved her time in Lawrence at the University of Kansas. I talked to her most nights, and we both cried when we received our first month's phone bills. We realized how much beer money traveled through the seventy miles of telephone lines. Despite our fun, we missed each other a great deal and were ready to journey from one campus or the other to spend time together. A month passed since we'd seen each other last, and our hearts and other parts missed each other.

She astounded me with stories of her new-found friends and their propensity to party. Though I hadn't met any of them yet, I knew them well—their likes, dislikes and idiosyncrasies driving Diane out of her mind. It was a wonder any of them passed any of their classes. Diane and I made bets on which ones would be gone at the end of the first semester, my money going on a skinny waif named Lori from Michigan. Diane thought Lori was a borderline alcoholic and a nymphomaniac. In three weeks she'd slept with four different guys, though she clung to a boyfriend of two years who remained working back home in Detroit.

My jealous thoughts burned low during these conversations like smoldering embers on an abandoned campfire. They flared to a dull flame after I'd tipped back a few too many and fought the urge to pick up an unattached girl at the bartender's last call.

Luckily, I lived with Mike who brought home some beauty queens to discover they turned into wart-ridden trolls come the light of morning. After the first week, I went to Walmart and bought a pair of earplugs. I spotted some of these creatures slithering out, hair disheveled, and no make-up covering the teenage acne as they took the walk of shame. Those women bolstered my resolve to stay faithful to Diane more than anything else.

Still, in the wee small hours of the morning, I would stand in the crowded bar and endure this sensation of being utterly alone, wondering what she was doing at the time. Was she also in the crowded confines of a local pub thinking of me, missing me, wanting me? Or was she too busy fighting off the advances of drunken behemoths who wanted to get into her pants? This long-distance romance started to suck.

An occasional thought flittered through my head that perhaps it wouldn't last. After all, it was a virtual smorgasbord of women ripe for the taking. Was I ready for this self-imposed chastity? I loved Diane so much, but it got tougher and tougher to tell if it was my love for her keeping the flames alit or my jealous desire for nobody else to have her.

After a solid month away from home, my father threatened to cut off funding if I didn't come back for a visit. I packed my suitcase full of dirty laundry and headed back to Kansas City after my 2:30 physics lab. Diane's Art Appreciation class ended at 4:30, and she planned to meet me at home afterward. We would eat dinner with our families, visit for as little time as possible and head out on the town to be alone. I bounced in my seat with excitement as I rolled down the highway.

CHAPTER TWENTY-FIVE

To quote Dorothy in her heartfelt desire to return to the place of her birth from the hellish freakiness of the Land of Oz, there's no place like home. When I rolled off I-435 onto Midland, I realized how much I missed my home turf. Though barely a month had passed, it seemed like a year as I cruised the old haunts. The Quick Shop, where we stopped on our way to anywhere to pick up sodas and snacks; the Sub n' Stuff which was open into the early morning hours to curb the post-drinking hunger; and the park where Diane and I smooched the hours away under the cover of a large oak tree all brought back fond memories.

The long grass at my house was a sign nobody cut it since I left, a chore I'm sure my father delegated to Jake in the futile hopes of getting the slug to earn his keep. I pulled into the driveway and parked behind Jake's clunker. I smelled something grilling in the backyard and my mouth watered. After a month of eating fast food and the slop dished out at the dorm, I was primed for a home cooked meal prepared by the talented hands of the woman who brought me into the world.

Before I could clear the front fender, my mother shot out the front of the house like a human cannonball and clutched me in a massive bear hug. She cried out something unintelligible and gave me another squeeze.

"Geez, Mom," I said. "You'd think I'm on leave from the army or something."

She cupped my face. "Oh, Jack, I'm happy to see you is all. This place hasn't been the same since you left. You look thin."

We walked toward the house with my backpack over one shoulder and Mom's arm over the other. I was in a modern day Leave It to Beaver, and June walked Theodore into the house.

"How's things at work?" I asked.

"Same old, same old," Mom said as we climbed the front steps. She stopped, troubled. "Your dad and Jake have been at war since you left."

"How come?"

"Well, since you went off to college, I think your dad wants Jake to get his act together and make something of himself. He's afraid Jake's going to be living at home until he's forty."

I rolled my eyes in irritation. This was all I needed. The dinner scene unfolded before me like an ominous premonition. After pumping me for information about how classes were going, Dad would comment how proud he was of me and make a comparison to my engineering studies and Jake's studies on how to flip burgers for five bucks an hour. Jake would howl in protest how the old man wouldn't get off his back, he held a job and he was responsible. Mom would try to intervene by making the comment that not everybody was meant to go to college, and Jake did the best he could. Jake would again howl, this time making some reference that his parents thought he was stupid. Dad would make some unreasonable demand on Jake resulting in Jake storming off, getting in his car and tearing away. I wondered if I should move my car to the other side of the driveway to save some time and perhaps a fender.

The house was filled with the wonderful aroma of fried potatoes, garlic, and a baking apple pie along with the sublime bouquet of marinated meats on the grill out back. The old man was a master with the charcoal and could whip fantastic creations on the grill which would flip even the staunchest of vegetarians into slobbering carnivores. He came in the back door, adorned in his cheesy Father's Day apron proclaiming "Don't Mess with the Chef" and wrapped me in a bear hug.

"How's my college boy?" he asked. Over his shoulder, Jake leaned back in a lawn chair rolling his eyes. It started already and I hadn't even set my backpack on the floor.

"Great, Pop. How's it going here?"

"Well, you know, same old, same old. Work, taxes and babysitting your older brother."

I was tempted to say something right there and nip this battle in the bud before it turned into a war of the wills with me stuck in the middle of the battleground, trying to get each side to wave the surrender flag. They could have their war, just after the weekend when I would be safe back on campus. Instead, I kept my mouth shut.

The old man pushed me to the door. "Come on out back."

Jake's shirtless frame sunk into a lawn chair, reading his latest issue of Car and Driver, his sockless ankles shaded green from the fresh cut backyard grass. He must have been on his mandated union break before tackling the front yard. I was surprised Dad squeezed any work out of him at all.

"What's up, Jake?" I asked.

"Hey," he said, eyes locked on the magazine. Jake's shirt hung off the back of the chair. His chest and arms were still tawny, but more defined than when I left. I'd lay money I could still best him on the bench press, but he'd made remarkable progress over the last month.

"Been hitting the weights, haven't you?" I asked.

He glanced up at last. "Pretty hard. Been working out with Don Miller."

"Well, you can tell. Your chest doesn't look like the Grand Canyon anymore."

Jake flexed, hopped from the chair and gave me a quick but sincere hug, clapping me twice between the shoulder blades.

"He's been lifting alright," my dad said from the grill. "I think it's been more beer cans than weights lately."

"Come on, Dad," Jake said, his rare, bright demeanor decimated. They'd obviously traveled this path before. "Can you lay off for one night?"

"Sorry, Jake," Dad said. "Didn't mean to upset you again. Your brother probably doesn't know how you've been spending your nights."

The knuckles on Jake's balled fists flashed white. "Well, I'm sure you'll tell him."

I was unsure of how to react to the whole situation. For as long as I could remember, things were a little tense between my father and my brother, but nothing on this level. Anyone with half a brain would feel the tension. I hoped the explosion could wait until I left for the weekend. Jake shot daggers with his eyes into the old man's back and stalked back into the house.

"You want sauce on your chicken, Jake?" Dad asked.

"He went inside, Dad." I moved beside him. Despite

the tense situation between my dad and my brother, my appetite flared like gasoline thrown onto a raging fire at the charcoal smell of the meat cooking. Dad tossed the tongs to the side, his nostrils flaring wide.

"I don't know what I'm going to do with him," he said, searching for an answer in the clouds above. "He's been partying more than he's been working. Hanging out with a group of nimrods who will never get past fry cook at McDonald's. I'm worried about him."

"Have you talked to him?" I asked.

"He won't listen to me. Just gets up and goes to his room or out to his car to cruise around."

"Well, Dad, maybe you should try talking to him instead of berating him all the time."

"I've tried," he said. "It doesn't do any good. He goes ballistic. I hoped you could talk to him, knock some sense into him."

"Since when does Jake listen to me?"

"Are you kidding? He's always admired you," Dad said.

"What? How many beers have you drank today? Jake can't stand me."

My dad's eyebrows shot up. "No, Jack, he looks up to you and what you've done. You're in college, you have the friends, Diane and a bright future. What does he have? A couple of loser buddies who'll probably do time in jail, a piece of shit car he works on but doesn't run right, no girl and a crappy job at a discount department store. What does he have to look forward to? He's lost in the dark and I can't find the light for him."

At first, I thought he unloaded his problem on me, but after a silent moment, the thought crept into my head he wanted help. My dad became oil to Jake's water once Jake hit his teens, acting as the unrelenting disciplinarian. They long ago began chopping at the ties once holding them close and were now hanging on by a thread. I realized Dad looked to me to help bridge the gap and sought my advice. It took me a minute to figure out what to say.

"Dad, you can't make Jake live up to whatever dreams you've set for me. He's going to have to figure out his own way, and you've got to try to give him the space to do that. Slamming him each time you speak to him isn't going to accomplish anything. It just shuts him down."

Dad grilled in silence, moving the chicken and the bratwurst around on the grill. Deep lines of worry etched in his aging face as he struggled to come to grips his oldest son wasn't going to be a Rhodes scholar.

"I don't know how to talk to him anymore," he said at last. "I don't know how to reach him."

"Maybe you should try being his friend," I said. "Be his father and his friend. I know you can because that's how you've always treated me."

At last, a faint smile broke across his face. "You going to be an engineer or a psychologist?"

"Well, maybe an engineer with a psychology minor."

He laid the tongs on the grill and embraced me, patting the back of my head.

"I think you could do anything you set your mind to," he said.

"Maybe you should try telling that to Jake, Pop."

He pulled back and held me by the shoulders, his eyes shimmering with what I'm sure was a mixture of pride, love and lingering frustration over his oldest son. I went back into the house and noticed Jake on the steps, head hanging like a worn out, beaten dog. I ticked my head toward the back door for Jake to go talk to our father. He groaned and climbed off the steps. I patted his shoulder as he passed by, apprehension filling his acne-scarred face.

Inside, Mom wrangled me into a kitchen discussion of school and her job, staying far from the topic of what transpired in the house during my absence. While we talked, I glanced to the backyard and saw Dad and Jake talking. I don't know if what I said to Dad had any impact or if the family's missing link coming home opened the channels of communication. However, in the end they laughed, their voices rising and filling the kitchen. The way the tension melted from my mother's face told me it was something neither of the men in her life did in quite a while. When I checked the yard again, my father hugged Jake in the same way he held me minutes before. It was enough to bring tears to even the toughest of eyes.

CHAPTER TWENTY-SIX

Diane and I drove for hours around the streets of Shawnee and into the surrounding neighborhoods of Lenexa, Overland Park and Merriam. Cruising in the car, letting the warm fall night breeze caress our cheeks through the open windows of my Mustang as I held her hand and stroked her long, supple neck, was priceless. I didn't realize how much I missed her until her beautiful face arrived at my door. She hugged me like a wife would hug her husband who returned from a lengthy tour of duty.

"You look awesome, Diane," I said as we waited at a stoplight near our old high school.

"So do you," she said. "I missed you."

"I missed you, too." The light turned green, and I gunned the car through the intersection. "Let's make a promise we won't go so long again without seeing each other."

"Deal," she said. "It's weird though. Even though I missed you, it wasn't like constant. I would go through periods where I wanted to see you so bad it hurt, and others where I was so busy with stuff I didn't even really think about you. You know what I mean?"

Her last statement might have caused a lot of guys to bring the car to a screeching halt, leaving smoking skid marks on the macadam. They would spin with a red hot fiery rage and demand to know what the hell that kind of comment meant. But, I knew what she meant. I'd be lying if I said it didn't jab my ego a bit to know I wasn't on the top of her mind twenty-four hours a day. However, we'd been together too long to lie to each other.

"I know what you mean." We pulled into the Shawnee Mission Northwest parking lot, empty save for a beat-up Malibu and a Buick on the far side of the lot toward the darkened soccer fields. I climbed out of the car, and Diane followed suit. Our hands interlocked as we walked the sharp decline toward the football field.

She squeezed my hand. "Does it bother you? That I didn't think about you all the time?"

"Well, I'd be lying if I said it didn't inflict the slightest bit of damage to my fragile male ego. But, I know what you mean because I did the same thing."

We reached the bottom of the hill and passed through the swinging gate leading to the football field. At midnight, the stands crouched in darkened silence. A scant amount of the parking lot's dim yellow light cast a faint glow on the playing field, the fuzzy white yard markers marred by the onslaught of cleats, balls and tumbling bodies from last night's practice. Once in the end zone, my monstrous hit on Number 24 from last year echoed, and the blood and sweat from years of practice sang. Echoes of Coach Utt's voice boomed over the crack of pads telling us to get our asses in gear or we would run laps until we puked.

"Is it a bad thing, Jack?" she asked, breaking me from the flashback.

"What?"

"Not always thinking about each other. You don't think it

means we're growing apart, do you?"

"No, it means we should be having more sex," I said, pulling her close.

She thumped my chest. "I'm serious. I mean, I don't think it's necessarily a bad thing."

"Nope. I can't study if I think about you. In fact, when I study in my room, I have to lay your picture face-down so I can concentrate."

"You're such a liar," she said.

"No, I'm serious, ask Mike." I wasn't lying, either. Before she'd left for college, Diane gave me a picture her friend Tracy took of her by the pool in her stark white bikini. Diane struck a provocative pose with her long, golden legs curled underneath, her smile jumping from the picture begging me to come and get her. I would catch myself salivating at the shot, and it would take Mike beaning me in the head with a balled piece of paper from across the room to break the spell. The picture was so good I caught four guys from across the hall of the dorm drooling over it like starving dogs eyeballing a piece of the master's steak.

"I don't expect to be on your mind every waking moment of the day, Diane. That's absurd considering all the other stuff we have going on. It doesn't mean we love each other any less. You're mine and I'm yours, forever."

"Forever?"

"Can you handle it?"

"Oh," she said. "I think I can manage."

We walked onto the field, and I realized I could conjure a football story for each yard marker we crossed. As we approached mid-field, whatever light thrown off by the parking lot dissipated at the thirty-yard line. In the spot where I'd watched many a coin toss, I pulled her close and kissed her, soft and full of longing.

I wrapped my arms around her tiny waist. "You know what? I missed out on something in high school."

"What was that?"

"I never got to nail the prom queen on the fifty-yard line."

She smacked my arm. "Hey, I was the prom queen and we did so much nailing we could have built the Eiffel Tower faster than the French."

"But, not on the fifty-yard line. I hear there's something about making love to the prom queen on the field of battle."

She popped open the first button on my jeans, eyebrows arched. I reached underneath her denim skirt and caressed her smooth flesh. Her eyes narrowed seductively with a slow lick of her sensuous lips, I don't think I ever wanted her more.

"Well, Mr. Touchdown, now's your chance," she said.

As we lay on grass damp from the late evening dew, we slipped from our clothes. We made love under the stars, eyes locked, each thrust pure magic. In a flash, the accomplishments I'd made on the football field seemed insignificant. I thought I'd experienced my last hurrah on that field, but I was wrong. The only thing missing was the cheer of the fans.

The Sunday night lights of downtown Manhattan were both inviting and depressing. On one hand they represented another semi-lengthy departure from Diane while on the other a welcoming beacon to my new world. As I crossed the rutted brick streets, bouncing over the dips in the road, I was hit with the same regret I experienced too many times during the semester, the regret I didn't go to KU with Diane.

As I pulled into the parking lot to the dorm and searched for a parking spot amongst the many junk heaps driven by my fellow freshmen, it hit me the emotion in play wasn't regret, but fear. Being yanked apart by a hundred miles strained the fiber holding our relationship together. And while we were so sure of each other on the football field a mere forty-eight hours earlier, I didn't have the same certainty when we were apart. Maybe it was my immaturity or paranoia raising its ugly head again. Whatever it was, its bitterness left its mark on my psyche and scared the living hell out of me.

CHAPTER TWENTY-SEVEN

Near the end of the semester in the spring of 1988, I attended a fraternity party with Mike and a guy he befriended in his freshman lit class. The guy was a pledge at the Kappa Sigma fraternity and raved about some bash at their house over the coming weekend. Mike couldn't manage to sit still for more than a minute waiting for Saturday night to roll around. We heard stories of the fraternity parties, but hadn't attended one. Images of togas and drunken debauchery flooded my brain, but I was pretty sure they came from the movie *Animal House* translated to the modern era.

Our dorm floor at Haymaker was pretty cool, and we even managed to sneak a keg up the back stairs a couple of times. Kyle Zabrosky, a giant we called Ogre who was the backup center for the football team, hoisted the metal barrel of fun over his shoulder and tromped seven flights of stairs without so much as a hitch. The second time we threw a party, Kyle traveled with the team to Oklahoma and it took several of us running in shifts to lug the hunk of metal up the stairs without giving ourselves hernias.

We thought the guys in the dorm were pretty cool and even a bit crazy, but after hitting this fraternity party, the Kappa Sigs made our Haymaker crew look like mischievous boy scouts at worst. Beer flowed like water—literally a few times when they doused the tile floor of their basement to determine who could slide the farthest. Some guy they called Doc won with a taped distance of twenty feet three inches.

There was Goliath, the two-story beer bong nobody at the party ever finished. The thing held two and a half pitchers, and you filled it from the second-floor bathroom window. The tube was under so much pressure they made a valve at the bottom of it. I tried it once and think more beer shot out of my cheeks than went in my stomach. A muscle-bound guy named Titan sucked the beer bong within inches of empty, but seconds later puked a gallon of suds in the sandpit.

They served trashcan punch comprised of grain alcohol and cherry Kool-aide, and it was so out-of-control the actives assigned a pledge from the house to dish the stuff out and make sure nobody with a cigarette came within ten feet. There were Jello, Slippery Nipple and Kamikaze shots free for the taking.

The music was loud and blaring and delicious to the senses. Jimmy Buffett was the preferred artist of the house as someone told me he was a Kappa Sig. But there were also goodies like Aerosmith, Zepplin, Def Leppard, and Rush among others. Some poor pledge popped in George Michael as a joke. When "Teacher" came on, the actives pummeled the kid about the head and shoulders, and gave him a week of cleaning the bathrooms and orders to relieve the poor schmuck at the trashcan punch barrel.

There was beer, partying and a tantalizing bevy of sorority girls shouting the well-renowned mating call of "I'm sooooo drunk." Mike was like a starving fat kid in an unattended candy store. His good looks and natural charms were no match for these poor ladies. He wandered off with at least three different girls that night.

As for me, I was a good boy, though it was only through sheer willpower and the thought of an ice-cold shower when I got back to the dorms. I hung out most of the night with the pledge chairman of the house, a guy named Benny Hunt, a gregarious guy who knew everyone at the party. Benny was slight with a head of receding, thin blonde hair in its last stages of the life cycle.

"Having a good time?" he asked, handing me another beer. I'd lost count, but was pretty sure I'd be puking before the night's end. I'd already consumed more beer in the two hours we'd been there than on any other night in my life.

"Definitely," I said. "You guys do this every weekend?"

He smacked a passing coed he said was his girlfriend on the butt. "Hell, no, this is one of the bigger ones, but not the best. Red Dog is the humdinger."

A blonde with cantaloupe breasts mashed to her chin staggered to us. "Benny, have you seen Marcy?"

She offered me a strange, squinty-eyed stare, like I wouldn't quite come into focus.

Benny pointed behind him. "Check out back by the sandpit. Sarah was holding her head while she was puking."

"Thanks," the blonde said before stumbling off in the opposite direction of where Benny pointed.

"I think she liked you, Jack," he said.

"Yeah, right. I don't think she could even see me."

"You should go after her and help her find Marcy. On the way, feel free to take her by Room 5."

I waved him off. "Thanks, Benny, but I don't think my

girlfriend would appreciate it much."

"Girlfriend? So that's why you've been hanging out with me all night. Why isn't she here?"

"She's in Lawrence," I said, mumbling the excuse for some reason, like I made up my relationship.

"A Jayhawk?" he said, incredulous. "You're dating a goddamn Jayhawk? Oh God, that makes my stomach hurt, dude. How long have you been going out?"

"Since we were eight."

Benny was caught in mid-drink and spit beer over me with his disbelief. "Since the eighth grade? Oh my God."

"No, dude. Since we were eight years old."

Benny dropped his full beer on the floor, and the plastic cup bearing the Wildcat logo rolled against my feet. He walked three or four steps away and pounced back, grabbing my shirt and pulling me close.

"What is wrong with you, man? Since you were eight? That's like…ten years. My friggin' parents weren't even married for that long. Hell, my dad wasn't married to his first *and* second wives that long."

I raised my eyebrows with a slight shrug of the shoulder. It was a move I'd perfected over the last few years when met with similar occasions of disbelief.

"I love her," I said. It was all I could say.

Benny picked up his cup and poured himself another beer. "Man, I couldn't do it. How can you stay on the beaten path with all this trim running around?"

I watched a stunning brunette bat her eyes at me before bouncing off to the backyard. "It's hard. But, you understand. You've got a girlfriend, right?"

"Yeah, but I'm a senior, dude. I sowed my wild oats for six years here. I'm getting ready to graduate so it's time to settle."

"Six years?"

"I changed my major a few times. The point is, Jack, you have your whole college life in front of you. Do you really want to trudge around campus with a hundred-mile ball and chain attached to your ankle?"

I never thought of Diane as a ball and chain. Never. As a redhead with the greenest eyes and tightest butt I'd ever seen stumbled forward, called me Tom and grabbed my hand, dragging me into the recesses of the house to find her friend Jeanine, Benny called out after me.

"Room 5, Jack. Right at the end of the hall."

I'm proud to say I stayed the course that night. The redhead searching for Jeanine passed out before we even reached the end of the hall on the first floor. I slung her over my shoulder and carried her out to the formal living room, plopping her on the couch.

I made my way through the now trashed halls of the fraternity house, peeking into the rooms looking for Mike. It was loud, rambunctious and fun. As I meandered around the house, even receiving a random kiss from some girl as she walked by giggling to herself, I found myself limping. I thought I might have torqued my ankle carrying the redhead to the living room. As I passed the open door to Room 5, I also wondered if it wasn't a psychological ball and chain pulling at my feet.

CHAPTER TWENTY-EIGHT

The longer our freshman year went on, the more time Mike and I spent at the Kappa Sigma house. The party pretty much sealed the deal for my lecherous best friend. Thus far, I stayed true to Diane though the temptations were bountiful, especially at the fraternity house.

We still liked the guys at our dorm and hung out in the halls with them, but it was like trying to compare a church ice cream social with an Aerosmith concert. The folks at the social may do their best, but it was doomed from the start as far as comparable entertainment value.

Right before the end of the semester, Mike and I went to the house for dinner one night and talked with Benny in his room. The lone furniture in the room were a couple of overhead beds with desks underneath, both devoid of any signs of books or papers, and a dirty green beanbag in front of a squat refrigerator with a television on top. Studying was a lost art with Benny. He'd been in college for six years, having switched majors a whopping seven times before settling upon Parks and Recreation Management. We drank a few beers, talked school, girls, and the expectations of a fraternity pledge while his roommate Max worked on the valve of the majestic Goliath beer bong.

It didn't take a lot of convincing on Benny's part we were Kappa Sig men at heart, and we duly signed over our commitment to the house on pledge cards. We celebrated with shots of tequila that tasted like Benny strained the amber liquid through a K-State basketball player's sweat sock after a grueling three-hour practice.

The only downer to our joining the fraternal ranks was the complete lack of excitement from anyone outside of the Kansas State campus. My parents worried my grades would suffer since I would be drinking beer twenty-four hours a day. I omitted the tidbit about the Kappa Sig's stocking the house's basement vending machine with beer. They both brought up my mom's cousin, Darryl, who was a most promising pre-med student on an academic scholarship prior to his joining the Sigma something fraternity. Now, he's a gas station attendant at a truck stop off I-80 in Nebraska, living with a skank named Susie and three snot-nosed, ill-mannered and mangy kids in a trailer park. My rebuttal that his manic depression and alcoholism played more of a factor than the fraternity house didn't assuage my mom's skepticism.

Diane's mouth said she was fine about the fraternity thing, but her body language said something else. She couldn't complain too much as she belonged to a sorority at KU. But, I'd known her long enough I could read between the telephone wires.

"I don't have a problem with it, Jack," she said. "I've just been to a couple of those parties and know how those girls act."

"I've seen it firsthand. Mike has definitely enjoyed the experience."

"Have you?" she asked.

I leaned back in my seat, surprised. "No way. Ask Mike.

Your Jack has been a good boy, haven't I Mike?"

"A goddamn saint, Diane," Mike shouted from across the room toward the outstretched phone. "I think he's going for priesthood."

"See? Nothing to worry about."

"Yet," she said. Static filled the line and I could tell she wasn't in the best of moods anyway. She had trouble with her biology and needed to nail the final to squeak out a top grade. "I miss you, Jack. That's all."

"It's only another week, and we can hang out during break."

We talked for another twenty minutes while Mike made gagging sounds in the background. I kicked his chair as I walked by making him mess up a drawing of a hydrocarbon compound. When I hung up, Mike tossed his pencil on his desk and faced me, his thin lips pressed together.

"So, how is this going to work, Chief?"

"What are you talking about?" I snagged a Nerf football and tossed it across the room. He snatched it from the air and winged it back to me.

"You know what I'm talking about. You and Diane and the hundred miles between you."

"This again? Man, it hasn't been a problem yet."

"Yet. Four years is a loooong time, brotha," he said, his wide mouth scrunched tight and eyebrows raised again in the patented Mike Washington look of disbelief.

"We've been together for ten, dude. Another four isn't going to kill us."

He caught the football and twirled it around in his dexterous hands, biceps flexing and dark hair hanging just over his eyes like one of those California surfer boys. He was built for the college life.

"I love Diane, man," he said. "You know that. But, I watched you at the party the other night. Girls hit on you right and left. You could have had the pick of the litter."

"So?" I didn't like where this headed.

"So? You really think you're going to be able to keep the pony in the stable for the next four years when there's all this pasture to explore?"

I contemplated his question. His bright eyes probed my face for any crack in the dam. He loved Diane like a sister, and the three of us had a great time when we were together. But, he also wanted someone to share the college experience with who wasn't already married.

I had to tell him the truth. "I'm sure."

He searched my face for a moment before throwing the football back at me. "Shit, I was afraid you would say that."

He turned back to his chemistry book, and I went back to my economics, visualizing the words and symbols on the page, but unable to concentrate on them. Keep the pony in the stable. I hoped Diane and I built a strong enough fence over the years because Mike was right on one thing. There was an awful lot of lush, green pasture out there.

CHAPTER TWENTY-NINE

I blinked and my freshman year was gone. Mike and I both made it through with a grade point average above 3.0, though my dad expressed some disapproval with my Calculus and Financial Accounting grades. I suppose I could have studied harder for both, but there were some killer parties at the Kappa Sig house the night before major tests in both classes. I'm lucky I could scrawl my name the following morning much less make a decent grade on the tests. I made the obligatory promise to try harder next semester.

Diane cruised through her first two semesters with a perfect row of A's lining her report card. Her mother beamed when I came to pick her up for our first date of the summer. She held her grade card in her hand with reverence like it was one of the original Ten Commandment stone tablets. Mr. Riven shook my hand and begrudgingly asked how school went for me like his wife ordered him to be polite, but turned his attention back to his newspaper before I finished answering.

We hit the town and cruised around to our favorite old haunts, running into various other people from our high school out on summer break. The high school kids still hung out at the Quik Trip off Metcalf, and we made a quick pass through there. I nipped our visit in the bud when I glimpsed Renny Hanks in the parking lot, hunkered on the hood of a dilapidated Camaro, drinking a beer with a couple of other derelicts whose names I couldn't remember. Renny spotted me and started to rise. I hit the gas before his widening tush could even clear the front fender. Diane didn't say a word.

I couldn't wait to spend some quality time with Diane. The phone calls over the last month grew longer in duration but fewer in frequency, and those seeds of doubt about the longevity of our relationship sprouted some tenuous fibers. I knew the summer would get rid of them for good.

Mike and I talked Eduardo into letting us work at the Bronze Café over the summer. He had a full-time staff, but let us fill in where possible. Sometimes it was our old Hobart Engineer jobs, sometimes slopping food in the kitchen and sometimes bussing the tables in the restaurant. We didn't care. We were happy to pocket a little spending money for the coming semester.

There were the revolving summer parties, depending on whose parents went out of town. Bobby Tuscari was the keeper of the schedule, but failed to book one at his own house. There hadn't been another Tuscari party since the one where I'd gotten my ass kicked by Diane's would-be suitor. He'd been grounded for two months after the cops busted the party, and ninety percent of Mrs. Tuscari's china broke in a fight between a couple of sophomores and one hundred percent of Mr. Tuscari's ample liquor cabinet disappeared.

Mike managed to find a steady girl to date over the summer, a diminutive redhead named Cindy Saunders. Cindy was a senior at Shawnee Mission South and a hostess at the Bronze Café. Mike charmed her from the get go, but promised me it was strictly a summer romance since she was heading for the University of Florida. I ignored his pointed barbs that long distance relationships just didn't work.

Things between Dad and Jake settled to some degree, the two of them acting at least amenable to each other when I was around. Jake dropped the Bargain Barn and flipped burgers at the Wendy's up the street, and even took a second job working days in the UPS warehouse.

"Two jobs, Jake?" I asked. "Color me impressed."

We hung out in his room, an absolute pit of dirty clothes, rock posters and pin-up girls. The smell of grease and sweat alone made me want to puke.

"Hey, anything to get the hell out of here," he said.

"Dad been riding you?"

"Not too bad. Whatever you said to him on your first visit home helped. Ever since I took this second job I hardly see them anyway. Don Miller and I are saving up to get an apartment together."

"That'd be sweet for you."

"At least I won't have to tell the girls I meet I live at home with my parents. How's the action at K-State?"

I marveled at the moment. In my nineteen years on this planet, this represented our most in-depth conversation. It was like we were two normal, civilized human beings talking. He didn't call me names or threaten to pull the waistband out of my underwear. I had to admit it was pretty cool.

"It's like a buffet, Jake. A freaking smorgasbord of women to choose from. You'd like it."

He gazed into the distance over my shoulder as if imagining the possibilities. I think my folks would help him get to college if he wanted to go, but I think Jake figured high school sucked enough for him he didn't want to push the envelope any further. His vision to the things which could have been broke when my mom called us to dinner.

"Nah. I'd flunk out in the first semester," he said. "But, what a fun semester it woulda been."

He walked toward the door, clapping me on the back. As he walked out the door, I thought, in the not too distant future, my brother and I might actually become friends. Imagine that.

CHAPTER THIRTY

    Reality set in three weeks into the first semester of my sophomore year. To be truthful, I didn't study much in high school and still graduated with a 3.6 GPA. My freshman year of college wasn't much different. But, in the fall of 1988, college slapped me broadside across the face with a cold, hard fact—I wasn't as smart as I thought.

    The pisser, and perhaps a contributing factor to my grades no matter how much I'd protested to my folks that it wouldn't be an issue, was the fraternity heading into prime party territory. Mike and I abandoned the residence halls and set up shop in the Kappa Sigma house. Shop, of course, was a relative term since we didn't have our own rooms. The chapter president assigned each pledge a room with two active members. You kept your clothes there, and they provided a desk at which to study, but you had to sleep in the pledge dorm, a crammed assembly of bunk beds set among cinderblock walls and concrete floors. It wasn't bad in the summer, but an unseasonable chill settled upon the barren Kansas plains, and the nippy air blew through the open windows. Temperatures plummeted to the mid-forties, and our psyches braced themselves for the winter to come.

    "Man, close the window," I said to Charlie Grant, an unfortunate pledge who drew the short straw to sleep by the window, his portly frame bundled in blankets.

Charlie didn't bother to flip over. "Can't. Fire code."

"What?"

"Fire code," Dewey Ray said from a bunk across the room. Dewey was a gangly lad from some dinky town in western Kansas, his mop of fire red hair in a perpetual state of disarray. "They got so many of us crammed in here, fire code says they have to keep the windows open."

"Jesus Christ," Mike said from the bed above mine. "You schleps believe that?"

"That's what Tank said," Dewey said. "You want to go ask him? Just remember, Eddie asked him, too."

The bed rocked as Mike settled back. I half expected him to jump to the cold, concrete floor and march out of the pledge dorm to go talk to Tank. Then again, we knew what Tank did to Eddie Ray. You wouldn't think sand would be so arduous to scrub off. I guess being covered in Elmer's Glue, rolled in the sand volleyball pit in the backyard in your underwear and made to stand at attention until the glue dried didn't help matters much. I'm sure the Greek system would technically call it hazing, but our actives called it an "Authority Education" session. Besides, Tank stood six-foot-eight, weighed three hundred pounds and had a nasty disposition. I didn't like to talk to him about anything.

Anyway, it wasn't the pending cold nights in the pledge dorm or the fact the actives in my room played more Tecmo Bowl on their Nintendo than studied that served as my reality slap. It was the fact my classes increased dramatically in their level of difficulty. The honeymoon was over.

Chemistry I turned to Chemistry II. Calculus evolved to Calculus II and made far less sense than its predecessor. Financial accounting surged to Engineering Economy. Classes went from the equivalent of a forty-yard dash to running the Boston Marathon, and I was apparently in no shape to run either race. I awoke from heart-pounding, sweaty nightmares where faceless men in black suits forced me to deliver my grade card into the waiting hands of my father with gigantic red F's running across the little piece of paper.

For four months, the classes didn't get any easier, and I failed to stop sweating about it. Diane and I shared the same physical space a grand total of five times over the course of the semester, and I studied so hard the constant ache in my brain made me worry a massive tumor grew unchecked in my noggin. I spent my life at the student union or the engineering lounge at Durland Hall trying to catch up. I'd spent the first three weeks partying with my new brothers before the realization about the coursework hit me. It took another couple of weeks for me to change my behavior and begin to buckle down. By then, it was like trying to stop the bleeding from a gaping chest wound with a cotton swab.

"At least you got an A in bowling," Jake offered as I trembled in his room during Christmas break.

"The sad thing is bowling is the reason I'm not on academic probation. Even the damn final was hard."

Jake huffed, but he had no frame of reference. I'd bombed my Calculus and Sociology finals and required an A in bowling to keep from dropping below a 2.0. Piece of cake, right? But, I was miffed at questions like "If you have a 6-10 pickup needed for a spare, over which board do you throw?" This teacher was a sadist to put crap like that on the final, but I managed to hold my A. I ended the semester with a 2.01 GPA, and my dad was going to bury his boot in my ass.

"He's going to kill me," I said.

Jake clapped me on the back. "Nah. He might beat the shit out of you, but he won't kill you."

There was a knock at the door and it creaked open. With my head in my hands, I peeked through the cracks of my fingers, much the way a scared kid does during a monster movie when he doesn't want to look but has to. It wasn't Frankenstein at the door, but the well-worn loafers of my father. He held my grade card in his hand.

"You and I need to talk," he said, eyebrows raised and lips pursed. "Now."

He stomped away, leaving the door ajar for me to follow him.

"Scratch what I said," Jake mumbled. "He is going to kill you."

I forced myself off the bed and headed out the door, wishing it had been Frankenstein, the Wolfman, or even Dracula clawing at the door. My fate in their hands would have been a piece of cake compared to what lay ahead of me.

CHAPTER THIRTY-ONE

In the spring semester of 1989, my classes didn't get any easier at Kansas State, but the studying did thanks to an absolute goddess named Brenda Rowland who some wonderful computer picked at random to help tutor me in physics. My dad said, in very clear terms, if I came home with another report card like the last, I'd be spending the next semester attending Johnson County Community College and living at home. He'd given me a few extra dollars for a tutor, and the system placed me with Brenda.

Brenda represented a unique challenge to me in a number of ways. First, this woman was jaw-dropping gorgeous. The kind of beauty that caused an ache in your chest when you looked at her. Her long, auburn hair hung below her well-defined, exercised shoulders. Her feline, emerald eyes captivated you and refused to let you go. Her full, supple lips left you wondering if they were as soft as they appeared, and a tight, compact body which would make any Victoria's Secret model green with envy. Mike turned into a drooling idiot when she was around. At least half the male population at K-State was after her, and for some strange reason, she locked her target on me.

The second challenging reason was my relationship with Diane veered a bit off the rails. Well, to be honest, the train was off the rails and barreling uncontrolled into a station packed with unsuspecting commuters. During the first half of the summer, Diane and I fell back into our old habits of being together. Despite the fact we both worked inordinate hours to earn money for school, we spent every spare moment with each other.

However, one stifling hot afternoon in August, as we heard the sounds of academia and beer beckon us from Manhattan, Mike and I headed to Oak Park Mall to find a birthday present for his girlfriend of the summer. Angelina was a sassy exchange student from Argentina who made your eyes pop out when she wore her skimpy, white bikini.

I drove along 95th Street heading toward the mall with Mike riding shotgun. "Dude, she is freaking awesome. You gotta bring her to Manhattan. The guys in the house will lose it."

Mike scowled like I'd suggested he bring some leper back home to meet mom and dad. "No way. One, any girl sees me with her and they'll forever be comparing themselves. I'll never get any action. Two, she goes home to Argentina in a couple of weeks anyway."

"But you're still getting her a birthday present? Color me impressed, Washington."

"Hey, we still have two weeks left, and if she ever comes back, I want her to remember me fondly enough she'll look me up."

Loitering teens and aged mid-day shoppers trying to stay out of the gagging heat and humidity packed the mall. We parked by Fun Factory and went in to play a few video games for old time's sake. I kicked Mike's ass in a rousing match of Street Fighter before he decided we should head out.

"What are you getting her, anyway?" I asked.

His face pinched in disgust. "Milli Vanilli."

"Aww, Jesus. Are you kidding me?"

"I wish. She loves the guys, for some reason. If she sings that *Girl You Know It's True* song one more time, I'm going to fire a bullet in my mouth."

We loitered around Spencer's, a novelty store holed up in the corner of the mall selling all manners of t-shirts, posters and gag items. For worst taste, we compared two current event t-shirts of an oil-soaked seal from the Exxon Valdez spill in Alaska and a bloody protest shirt with fake bullet holes which read "I went to Tienanmen Square and all I got was this lousy t-shirt". I was about to cast my vote for the Beijing massacre when Diane walked by the front of the store with someone at her side.

"Whoever made this Tienanmen Square shirt oughta be freakin' shot," Mike said as I darted past him. Something on my sonar pinged, a lone torpedo darting through the water to sink my ship.

Hurrying toward the entrance, I caught a glimpse of her black mane disappearing down the escalator with another dark head of hair—definitely male. I walked out of the store and Mike yelled after me, but I kept going.

"Jack," Mike called again, but I raised my finger to my lips to shut him up. I don't know why, but I didn't want Diane to know I was here.

Once I hit the bottom of the escalator, they disappeared into B. Dalton's bookstore. I followed and made my way to the back of the store, catching glimpses as she and her companion wandered the center aisles. The hardened ball in the pit of my stomach sunk lower to the point where nausea threatened to rear its ugly head.

I took cover by a display of my favorite author Stephen King's latest book The Dark Half, when Diane and her companion broke cover in the reference section. My heart hardened to match the exact consistency of the ball in my stomach at Diane's company. I don't know who I expected to see—perhaps some dork from one of her classes she ran into or even some handsome stranger leaving me to wonder how well they knew each other. But, it wasn't a dork or a stranger. It was Zack Hunter. The same Zack Hunter who I fought at Bobby Tuscari's party two years ago.

Mike caught up to me and opened his mouth to speak before he spotted Diane and Zack facing each other, Diane giggling at some book Zack held. I didn't know what could be so damn funny. They were in the Reference section for God's sake.

"Is that...?" Mike asked.

I cut him off. "Yeah, that's him."

"Jesus. What the hell is he doing here? What are you going to do?"

"You mean, am I going to run over there and start throwing haymakers at the guy?"

The thought had crossed my mind. Dart over there and shove Mr. Granite Jaw into the Romance section, sending blinding pink paperbacks tumbling across the aisles. Two years ago, I was pissed when I saw them together. Now, a deep pain ached in my chest. The ugly Jayhawk stitched on the front of Zack's shirt confirmed this wasn't an impromptu reunion.

"Jack?" Mike said, his voice a strained whisper.

"Let's get out of here." I stomped along the aisle and jostled a few innocent bystanders trying to peruse the magazine racks. Darting up the escalator, I headed as fast as I could to the parking lot. Mike's sneakers pounded the tile behind me, trying to keep up. With each step I took, the pain in my chest mounted, the ball in the pit of my stomach growing like a massive tumor on steroids.

Once I reached the sanctity of my car, I gripped the steering wheel tight and placed my sweating forehead against it. Mike climbed in the passenger seat and stared out the grimy windshield into the hot afternoon sun. My body flushed with nausea and fury, fighting the simultaneous urge to both throw up and hit something.

"Tell me I'm being paranoid, Mike," I said after a minute.

"Dude, I wish I could." It was the worst thing he could have said.

Back on campus, the scene in the mall played on an uninvited and continuous loop in my brain over the next several weeks. Diane told me later that night she went to the mall, but failed to mention with whom she shopped. I didn't press the issue and wasn't ready to hear the answer anyway.

My logical brain locked in the epic struggle with my embittered heart. My heart offered the hollow argument it was a chance meeting, but my brain called bullshit. Diane and I had been together for so long and shared so much I couldn't bring myself to believe she cheated on me. My imagination would overtake my brain and force it to envision illicit encounters between the love of my life and the womanizing Zack Hunter.

It was a most unwelcome flash of Diane and Zack locking lips on the dance floor in some Lawrence nightclub playing in my mind while I was supposed to be concentrating on my physics homework. A tap of a pencil from across the table brought me back to earth.

"Hello?" Brenda said, the corners of her gorgeous lips rising. "You there, Jack?"

"Huh? Oh yeah, I'm here."

She cocked her head to the right and narrowed those enthralling green eyes. "No, I don't think you are."

"I'm all yours, Brenda."

"Really?" she said, baring her gums as she leaned forward across the table. "Did you and what's-her-name breakup over the weekend?"

I blushed, my face a glowing red visible across the study tables at the K-State Union and into the far reaches of western Kansas. The little devil on my shoulder whispered of the temptations in which I should partake. Before me stood the apple in my own little Garden of Eden, an apple who wanted me to take a bite in the worst way.

Again, the picture of Diane and Zack, fabricated in my mind or not, flashed before me. This time, they moved from the dance floor of an unknown nightclub to the backseat of my own car. I almost yelled out loud to Zack to get off my girlfriend.

I shook myself back to reality. "No, Brenda. I'm not quite fair game yet."

She leaned back against the seat and folded her arms across her beautiful chest. "Well, I'm happy to hear the 'yet' part. It's a first."

Oh, God. What in the hell was I going to do? My girlfriend since I was eight eyeballed another guy with whom I'd duked it out over the same issue two years before while the most exotic girl on the campus of Kansas State University wanted nothing better than to take me back to her apartment and jump my bones. I was tempted let me tell you, so much so I figured I'd better keep my lower half hidden by the table for at least ten or fifteen minutes lest I embarrass myself.

My eyes tore themselves from Brenda, who should be tutoring me in physics instead of sexually torturing me, and focused back on my homework problem at hand. But, my brain could care less what coefficient of friction was required for the one-ton car to make it up a thirteen-degree slope at twenty miles per hour. My brain focused on the fact I was scared shitless. For the first time in my life, I wanted someone other than Diane.

CHAPTER THIRTY-TWO

At Christmas break of 1989, Diane and I were farther apart than ever. The management of the miles over the weekends wore thin on both of us. I was tired of talking to her on the phone, tired of leaving messages with her roommates, tired of driving back home to Kansas City so we could be together for a few hours before one of us headed back to campus for one activity or another.

The separation was tangible; you could almost reach out and grab it even when we were together. I'm sure Zack Hunter and legions of other would-be-suitors lined up outside Diane's door, waiting for opportunity to knock and let them in. In my own little world, Brenda chased after me with an admirable persistence. While she wasn't sitting home alone at night knitting while waiting for me to break up with Diane, she kept her options open and available.

Diane's spring formal the following semester was pure drudgery. It was a black-tie affair at some ritzy club in downtown Lawrence. I acted like a douche because it was black tie forcing me to shell out fifty bucks for a monkey suit I didn't want to wear and couldn't afford. Diane was perturbed I moped around for most of the night, but it was hard to get into the festive spirit when your girlfriend failed to acknowledge your existence. She fluttered around from table to table, dragging me along like some puppy dog on a leash. It was not the Diane I'd come to love more than life itself over the last eleven years. She acted like someone else.

The summer didn't improve things, and I couldn't wait for school to start again. Mike and I worked back at the Bronze Café, and Diane took a job at the Gap selling denim apparel to people with too much money to waste on clothes. Jake moved out of the house and lived with Don Miller while working two jobs so we didn't cross paths much. Dad stressed about a couple of contracts he lost to Dettinger & Son's Construction. Mom acted her cheery self, glad to have me home even though I didn't spend much time there.

However, I think I was with my mom far more than Diane. While I worked days at the Café, Diane worked nights at the Gap. The mall didn't close until ten o'clock, leaving little time for us to do anything together. We went out on the occasional weekend night when one of us didn't pick up an extra shift, but our interactions with each other were strange, almost fraternal. The crack in our relationship grew at an exponential rate, and I didn't know how to close it, if I wanted it to close or even if it could be closed.

In the fall semester of 1990, I watched the snow falling to the front yard of the fraternity house, the burnt orange sun dipping below the horizon. My calculus book screamed at me to study it, but I couldn't muster the energy. The final loomed in two weeks, and I was as prepared for it as I would ever be. From a grades standpoint, it would be my best semester yet, but from a personal level, it was the worst four months of my life. As the giant snowflakes fluttered and swayed in the December air, I realized the immensity of my loneliness.

The knock on my door broke me from my trance. I hoped it wasn't Billy Hunsacker wanting help with his chemistry again. I didn't think I could muster the energy to explain ionic bonds to him one more time.

"Come in," I said, swinging around in my swivel chair.

The door opened and Brenda walked in, dressed in a long skirt, powder blue sweater and carrying a package in her hands. Snowflakes clung to her long, dark hair, unwilling to melt or fall to the floor. The way she looked, I can't say I blamed them.

She stepped through the door and closed it behind her. "Hey, Jack. I brought you an early Christmas gift."

I was surprised to see her. Of course, I felt like a schmuck because I got her nothing, though the thought crossed my mind. I'd been at the mall and found a bottle of the perfume she wore that drove me out of my mind. But, buying a girl perfume would be a betrayal to Diane, so I walked away from the perfume counter empty handed.

Brenda slipped across the room, dropped to a chair and handed me a package wrapped in reflective, red paper with a shiny green bow squeezing the box. I opened the gift and found an ornate silver picture frame. Inside the frame sat a black and white face shot of Brenda, her long auburn hair swooping above her eyes and a delicate hand resting on her chin. I love black and white photos anyway, as I'm sure she knew by now, but I wasn't sure what I should do with it. I loved it, but I couldn't put it on my desk. The fact she'd given me a picture of her while she knew good and well one of Diane owned real estate on my desk didn't slip past me.

"You like it?" she asked, leaning into me. Her perfume,

the exact kind I thought of buying her, awakened a longing within me, a passion that buried its head for far too long. I was afraid to even look at her. Our heads were too close, and if I did look, I would kiss her.

"It's great, Brenda. What a great head shot of you."

"My dad took it this summer while we were at the lake. I was sunbathing on the dock when he comes strolling out with the new camera my mom bought him for his birthday."

As if it wasn't tortuous enough that Brenda huddled so close our arms touched, now I also dealt with the image of her in a bikini, lounging by shimmering lake waters. I wanted to turn to her, but couldn't force myself to do it. I still loved Diane, regardless how rough the last year was. I hadn't cheated on her once in our eleven years. But the image of her and Zack continued to haunt me. I didn't know with any certainty if there was anything going on between them. I wanted to believe in Diane, that she wouldn't do it to me, but I wouldn't bet my life on it.

"Jack?" Brenda asked.

It was said at such a low level, a whisper of a whisper, I wasn't sure if I'd heard it at all. Her minty breath danced on my cheek, and the last remnants of my resolve crumbled away as she placed a cool hand on my burning cheek. She turned my face toward hers, and her probing stare broke the water in the dam, releasing a desire I couldn't hold back any longer. She leaned in and our lips met in a soft, passionate kiss. As her mouth opened and our tongues met, twirling and intertwining, I didn't think I ever wanted anyone as much in my life.

I don't know how far we would have gone if Mike hadn't barged in to borrow some toothpaste. If he hadn't walked through the door, I don't know if I would have been able to do anything but take her to my bed.

"Oh…shit," he said, wide-eyed and mouth agape. "Sorry."

I don't know if his intrusion was welcome or not because as Brenda and I broke our kiss, I noticed the picture of Diane on my desk. The shame filling my face was matched in power by the lustful throbbing in my groin. Mike stumbled as he backpedaled out of the room and shut the door behind him. I turned back toward Brenda but leaned back out of the attack zone. She picked up on my non-verbal cue and pressed to her feet, following my initial glance toward the photo on my desk.

"Well, I guess I should get going," she said. "I just wanted to drop off the picture for you."

I rose, unsure of the proper etiquette at the moment. Part of me wanted to apologize for the kiss. Part of me wanted to explain my confusion at the moment. The part of me most men are forever accused of thinking with wanted to grab her in my arms and pick up where we left off, but the moment evaporated and we both knew it. Brenda wanted me, but I also knew she wanted me without the heavy strings attached to my eleven-year relationship.

"Thanks for the picture," I said, holding it in my hands. "It's great."

She took a few tentative steps forward, rose on her toes so her face evened with mine, and planted those supple lips against my red-hot cheek.

"So was the kiss," she said.

She sauntered out the door, glancing over her shoulder as she gave me a coy wink. I didn't follow her, awash with such a range of emotions I didn't know what to do. At last, I decided the best course was to sit before my legs gave way. Scant seconds later, Mike burst through the open doorway, shut it behind him and leapt across the room to the chair Brenda had occupied.

"Dude," he said. "Sorry to interrupt you."

"No, don't worry about it. Probably a good thing you did."

"I have to say I'm surprised."

I groaned and leaned back in my chair, my forearm covering my eyes, trying to mask my shame as if it lit my face in garish, pink neon. "I know. I'm a freaking scumbag, dirtball, cheating low-life."

"No. You're goddamn human, Jack. It's a modern miracle in biology you lasted this long. Besides, what do you have to be sorry about?"

"Cheating on Diane, for one," I said.

"Cheating is such an ugly word. Besides, it depends on your definition. All you did was kiss her for God's sake."

I groaned again and paced the cluttered confines of the room. Mike had a valid point, but it was hard to listen to a man with scruples the size of peas. I kissed another woman and wanted to do more, would have done more if we weren't interrupted. Whether it constituted cheating in my book or Mike's, I was pretty sure it would meet Diane's definition to a T.

"What the hell am I going to do?" I asked.

"I don't know, dude," Mike said, getting up with a heavy sigh and taking the picture of Brenda from my hands. He gaped at it for a moment before holding it up. "But, you're not going to be able to hold out from this much longer."

He handed me the picture and left the room, leaving

me to my guilt and shame. I stared at the phone and considered calling Diane, but knew I couldn't discuss this over the phone.

Ten minutes later, I hit the road to Lawrence. As my Mustang chewed the miles on I-70, the snow turned to a light rain plinking the roof in competition with the hum of the engine and the windshield wipers swooshing back and forth. I tried listening to the radio, but Paula Abdul or Phil Collins didn't cut it. When I tried another station and *You're Cheatin' Heart* blared through the speakers, I decided fate told me to drive in silence.

It was dark by the time I reached the University of Kansas, and I drove through the campus well below the posted speed limit, trying to devise some sort of explanation of what transpired in my room less than two hours ago. I envisioned Diane's shocked, tear-filled eyes as I confessed my sins. I couldn't keep this from her, no matter how much it hurt. She could read me like a book and would sense something anyway.

The lights from her sorority house shined in the distance. I drove with such dread I idled along the wet street. The massive white mansion with its giant pillars glowed with Christmas lights as I stopped in front. On the front porch, a couple stood by the door, holding hands and talking. The girl's face turned to the ground and the boy lifted her eyes toward his. She shifted from one leg to the other. At last, she gave in and kissed him, wrapping her arms around his neck and pulling him close. The front door opened and two girls emerged, breaking the couple from their embrace. The girl took several awkward steps back into the porch light and dropped her eyes to the ground.

I turned back to the road in front of me. My mind, minutes ago a jumbled mess of thoughts and emotions, was now a complete and utter blank. I took my foot off the brake and rolled forward, past the front of the house and back toward the highway. Minutes later, heading back toward Manhattan, the girl's face was on my mind, and I knew what she felt. After all, I could recognize the love of my life and Zack Hunter, even from the street through a rain-covered car window.

CHAPTER THIRTY-THREE

Christmas break neared an end. As much as I missed home, I welcomed the return to school for the next semester. I stalled talking to Diane about my encounter with Brenda and had no burning desire to bring up what I observed in front of her sorority house. Things between us were awkward enough and for good reason given the secret we both kept.

Wanting something to munch on, I ventured from my room. Jake made a rare appearance at our house for dinner, and he and Dad camped out on the couch watching some doughy bald guy, hopped up on drugs, running buck-naked around a convenience store on their favorite show "Cops."

Mom busied herself in the kitchen making Christmas cookies and watching 60 Minutes where they ran a segment on how offensive Madonna's *Like A Prayer* video was to the religious right. She hummed *Jingle Bells*, oblivious to the television, a happy little smile on her face. I slid to her side and slipped an arm around her waist.

"Jack," she said, acting surprised I'd ventured out to mingle with the commoners. "What brings you down?"

"I guess I'm hungry for one of those cookies."

She handed me one off a plate, and I popped it in my mouth, suppressing the urge to scream as the molten chocolate chips burned the roof of my mouth. She rolled the dough for a moment, and turned to me, eyes crunched with concern.

"You haven't mentioned a word on Diane's trip, honey. Aren't you worried about her being over there by herself?"

My radar went on red alert. She may as well asked me for a dissertation on the current state of foreign relations with the Middle East. My tired brain held the same amount of knowledge on both subjects.

"What are you talking about?" I asked.

"Diane's semester abroad in Europe," she said, eyes furrowed with incredulous belief I didn't know. To tell you the truth, I can't say I blamed her. You'd think the boyfriend would know his girlfriend was leaving for Europe for five months.

I didn't say a word, storming out of the kitchen, through the living room and out the front door. I sprinted across the street to Diane's house though clueless about what I would say. Why didn't she tell me? My mother must have heard the grapevine wrong.

At the front door, I sucked in a couple of exaggerated gulps of air to calm myself so I didn't pound the door off its hinges. I decided I couldn't ring the doorbell too hard, so I pressed the button and waited. Mr. Riven answered the door with his ever-present pipe in the mouth and Wall Street Journal in hand, disappointment dripping from his gaunt face.

"Mr. Riven, is Diane here?"

"No, Jack. She's working at the mall." His voice dripped with distaste for me, but at the moment I didn't care. "Her last shift, don't you know."

"No, I didn't know," I said, running back across the street. I hopped in my car and sped as fast as I could to Oak Park Mall without dragging an army of police cars with me.

I sped along I-435, clueless what I would say to her, my mind a whirlwind of emotions and random thoughts. The Brenda and Zack Hunter incidents weighed on my mind, and I knew we hadn't spent much time together over the winter break. But, why didn't she tell me she was going to freaking Europe for a semester?

When I rolled up to the mall, the doors were already locked which was a good thing because I would have stormed into the Gap and made one hell of a scene. Instead, I cruised to the back of the parking lot, found her car and waited. The longer I waited, the more the anger faded to pain. What hurt the most was part of me was glad she was going, the mechanics of our relationship made easier.

I studied the cracks in the dashboard, still trying to figure out what I should say when a knock at my window almost sent me through the roof of the car. Diane waited there with her thin eyebrows raised. She walked to the passenger side and climbed in.

"God, it's freezing out there," she said, the windshield holding her gaze instead of at me. "What are you doing here?"

"Do I need a reason to see my girlfriend?" I asked, my defensive tone sharper than I intended.

"No, I'm glad you came by. We need to talk and I didn't want to do it on the phone. God knows we've done enough of that lately."

We need to talk. The minute those words left her mouth, my stomach hardened to a cannonball as it would for any guy who heard the four shittiest words in the English language.

"Yeah, we do," I said, unable to meet her eyes.

We waited in awkward silence, and a million memories

flooded my brain like a movie on fast-forward—the tissue in her nose from the dodgeball incident which brought us together, myself jumping in front of her when Renny Hanks made his advances, the Christmas gift of the bra, on the swing in her backyard when we were kids, and the two of us alone in a little shack by the river on a farm in the middle of Nebraska—my personal favorite. Twelve years flashing by in the blink of an eye, and it was coming to an end.

"Jack, I don't know how to tell you this…"

"You're going to Europe."

She drew back in surprise. "Oh. You know."

"I heard it from my mother, thank you very much." My temper rose again and I flashed a molten glare that would've melted steel.

"I wanted to tell you a million times, but I couldn't think of how to do it or what to say, exactly. Besides, I only found out I was going for sure a couple of weeks ago. Oh, Jack, please don't look at me that way."

As pissed off as I felt, I couldn't take those blue eyes watching me, tears shimmering. I loved her and resisted the urge to take her in my arms, stroke her hair and tell her everything would be okay. We were done and such appeasements were gone.

"Is Zack Hunter going, too?" I asked.

"Why would you ask that?"

"Come on, Diane," I said. "You haven't lied to me before, don't start now. I know you've been seeing him."

She shifted in her seat, the wheels in her brain churning to come up with something to say. "He's going. A good portion of our French class is going, and he happens to be in it."

Ahhh, the nail in the coffin. While I would be slaving

away in the heartland of America, Diane would gallivant around Paris with Mr. Wonderful. I wanted to throw up. Tears and raw emotion tried to force themselves to the surface, but I pushed them back. I wouldn't cry in front of her at the end.

"When do you leave?"

"Wednesday. We fly to London and then to Paris. I'm staying with a French family with a girl my age."

"Sounds like it'll be a good experience for you." The words came out bitter, and I suppose I couldn't mask them. I knew this was coming for some time now, but it didn't make it any easier in the end.

"Can I write you?" she asked. "Let you know how it's going?"

"Sure, just don't mention anything Zack related, okay?"

She nodded. "Look, I've got to get home. Mom's holding dinner for me."

I said nothing, focused on a post in the emptying parking lot and the cascading snow swirling in its light on the lonely December night.

"God, it's over isn't it?" she asked, eyes cast to the floorboards, tears running down her face.

I reached over and wiped a hot tear away from her cheek. "I guess it really is."

She leaned over and gave me a lingering kiss on the cheek, pressing her face against mine. Her tears burned against my face, and it took every ounce of willpower to hold back my own. "I do love you, Jack Phipps. I always will."

She pulled the door handle and left the car. She hurried around the front, sobbing as she went. I slumped in stunned silence, the finality of it setting in. She started her car and drove away into the night. I don't know how long I watched the snow falling, the massive flakes accumulating on the hood of the car.

"I love you, too," I said at last, reaching forward and putting the car in drive.

CHAPTER THIRTY-FOUR

The next few years were nothing but a blur. I wish I could say they were happy times, but on the whole, it would be a lie. Brenda and I became an official couple after Valentine's Day. She was patient after Diane and I broke up. We lasted for a year before she graduated and moved to Michigan to work as a chemist for General Motors. We had a good time along the way, some good parties, a few laughs and some great sex, but Diane was forever stamped on my brain.

During our junior year, Mike hooked up with a girl he met at Last Chance named Stacy Dunbrooke. Though it started as a drunken one-night stand, she turned out to be the one for him. It was as if someone flicked a switch in his head telling him his bird-dogging days were over. There was nary a moment when those two peas in a pod weren't together. He kidded about my being the carefree bachelor and having to put up with their lovey-dovey schmoozing.

"Payback's a bitch, Jack," he said. I suppose he'd hung around with me and Diane enough over the years to earn the right to utter the phrase as much as he wanted.

Diane wrote me four times during her semester in Paris. True to her word, the name Zack Hunter didn't touch the page.

Over the summer break, I caught the two of them leaving her house. Diane with her head lowered as if something of incredible interest was on her shoes, while Zack puffed his chest toward my house. If he could've pissed on the tree in my yard to mark his turf he would have. What a douche bag. I couldn't understand what my ex saw in him, but it wasn't my problem any longer.

It felt strange spotting her at her house over the breaks or the occasional weekend without speaking to her. I don't know if she stole as many glances from her bedroom window as I did when I was home. I wanted to call her in one way but was afraid to in another. Would we have anything to say to each other after all this time?

The weekend before the winter break of my junior year, I cruised back home for a little quiet time to study for finals. There were some great pre-holiday parties going on at the fraternity house, and it was imperative I avoid temptation for a weekend. The deadline on a major project in my Industrial Design class loomed, and I needed some space to spread out and work.

I pulled off Midland Drive into my neighborhood and crunched over fallen leaves from the massive oak trees, the group Nelson belting out some ballad on the radio. Mike and Stacey invited me to go to the movie *Flatliners* with them, but the thought of being a third-wheel was too depressing so I declined.

As I turned the corner to my house, I saw the moving van planted in front of the Riven house. A couple of thick-necked men hauled out Mrs. Riven's prized piano while she watched them from the front bay window, chewing her nails. I pulled into my driveway and climbed out. Diane was moving. Despite my brain telling me to do otherwise, I crossed the street.

At the open front door, I let some gorilla with arms so furry you could have braided the hair slip by with a box labeled FRAGILE before I knocked on the wood frame.

"Hello?" I said. Mrs. Riven appeared from the living room, her worried look about the piano replaced with a gigantic smile.

"Jack," she said, wrapping me in her arms. "Oh, my goodness, how you've grown up. How are you?"

"Fine, I guess. What's going on here?"

"Mr. Riven landed a job heading a small law firm in Chicago, and we couldn't pass it up. Your mother didn't tell you?"

"No, she didn't." Count Jack as the last to know again.

"Well, we only found out last week. Are you looking for Diane? She's still at school."

I admit I was disappointed. A year passed since Diane and I spoke. We offered the occasional wave when we were both home at the same time, but her letters from KU ceased. I didn't tell anyone, including Mike, I still kept her picture in my desk drawer and snuck a peek at it on occasion, wondering what might have been. As great as Brenda was, she couldn't hold a candle to Diane.

"Oh, well I just got home and thought I'd take a chance. If you talk to her, tell her I said hi...and good-bye." Her mother furrowed her brow. She opened her mouth to say something, must have thought better of it, and closed it again. "Good luck, Mrs. Riven. I'll miss your cookies."

Tears welled in her eyes, and she wrapped me in a tight embrace. She pulled back and gave me a mother's kiss on my forehead, though my height forced her to pull my head low and stand on her tiptoes to do it.

"It breaks my heart to see you two broken up," she said.

"But not Mr. Riven," I said. She pressed her lips together and stepped away.

"No, not Mr. Riven, but, maybe you'll have a daughter someday and understand him a little better."

"Maybe. Well, good luck."

I walked to the front door, waited for the Gorilla to pass with another box and plodded home. Diane was moving away. Of course, she'd still be at KU in all likelihood, but any thoughts of us being together again now faded away.

"Jack?" Mrs. Riven said behind me. "You should call her. Talk to her."

I thought for a moment. Diane's mom and her wide, hopeful eyes made me want to run across the street and do that very thing. But, I didn't know what I would even say to her.

"I wish I could, Mrs. Riven," I said, heading back home.

CHAPTER THIRTY-FIVE

I graduated from Kansas State University with a degree in Industrial Engineering in December 1991. Four and a half years of sweat and toil rewarded by a diploma you didn't even get when you walked across the stage. My parents busted at the seams with pride. I was the first person in my family to graduate from college, and my dad grinned like a kid on Christmas morning. Even Jake gave me half a hug and said it was pretty cool—an intense show of emotion for him.

In the middle of January, I began my career in the engineering department at a small Kansas City manufacturing company called Kinnison & Sons. We made a number of things for the airlines, namely uncomfortable seat cushions with minimal padding, and they were desperate for someone to make their operation run more efficiently. I worked for a man named Charlie O'Brian, a thick-framed Irishman who loved to play poker in the lunchroom during breaks. I didn't know much about the game myself, but there were sharks swimming in those poker waters. A young guy named Johnny Chase offered to teach me the ropes but said I should stay away from the poker game until I learned how to swim. Johnny only worked a summer there before he quit going to K-State and became a successful poker pro.

I waited until I cleared my first couple of paychecks before I began apartment hunting. My mom and dad urged me to save some money and get a starter house, but I couldn't do it. I was twenty-two years old, making a nice chunk of change and couldn't freeload off my parents any longer. Jake lost one of his jobs and couldn't afford to live with Don Miller any longer. He was back home at the young age of twenty-four. I talked him into going to school and getting some sort of technical degree. My father even agreed to pay for it if he'd go.

In April 1992, I moved into an undersized, but livable two-bedroom apartment at Three Lakes off 119th Street in Overland Park. It was a bit of a grind to fight the traffic heading to downtown, but I liked the place which offered a great view of one of the lakes from the tiny balcony off my bedroom. In the morning, the ducks would swim in the swirling mist as the blood-red sun rose in the background. It was a good way to start the day.

Mike and Stacy got engaged over the summer, surprise of surprises. My best friend, the perpetual bachelor was going off the market. He was hook, line and sinker in love, and I couldn't be happier for him. They set a wedding date for the following year, and Mike had a growing list of the things he wanted for his bachelor party. I thought I'd have to take out a sizable loan with my bank to be able to afford it.

Socially, I kept a low profile the first year after graduation. I endured several blind dates which didn't amount to anything. A sweet secretary at the plant set me up with her daughter. Our relationship made it to the third date before she confessed she was still in love with her old boyfriend, a hopeless mechanic at a local garage named Denny, which worked out fine because I wasn't into her anyway.

For the most part, I played the leading role of a hermit on the weekends reading, playing on my new computer and wasting time watching *American Gladiators* on television. Every so often, I'd pull out the pictures of Diane and wonder what she was doing. Mike touched base with her on occasion and said she was still single and working as a high school French teacher at a school in western Kansas. Lucky kids out there, but I couldn't picture my Diane on the great Kansas plains.

The king of surprises from the first year out of college sprung in October while I walked the plant floor with the safety manager who wanted some help constructing some new guarding for a die-cut machine we'd purchased a week ago. My boss trained the operators on the machine's procedures, but I had a conference in Atlanta and missed the installation. The safety manager, Mindy Thomas, explained her trials and tribulations with one of the machine's operators. The guy acted abusive about the machine guards and rambled how he wouldn't be able to do his job, even though he'd only been working in the plant for the week I was gone.

"They must be pretty hard up for employees to hire this jack ass," Mindy said as we neared the machine. She was a thin, fiery brunette who was as serious as a heart attack about her job.

As we rounded a corner, the operator in question squatted on a stool reading a girlie magazine. It wasn't a nudie periodical, but a bar napkin had more material than these girls wore. Management could fire him for sexual harassment on the spot if Mindy chose to go that route.

"Well, here we are to make your life miserable once

again," she said as we approached the operator, a giant of a man with scarred hands the size of dinner plates. As he turned to us, I bit back the urge to scream in surprise at the leathery, pitted face of Renny Hanks.

"Well, holy shit," Renny said with a crafty grin and a tiny toothpick sticking out of the corner of his mouth. His yellow teeth revealed his dental hygiene hadn't improved over the years. "It is a small world."

I was as shocked as him. My wildest nightmares didn't entertain a scenario where I worked in the same place as Renny Hanks. I figured he would be dead or in prison by now.

"Hey, Renny," I said at last, terrified and thrown back in time to Mr. Gashinder's yard and Renny's fist raised to split my skull. The murder in his bloodshot eyes, the bark from the oak tree clawing at my back. I was half-tempted to check if Mr. Gashinder lingered around anywhere to save me once again.

Renny hadn't aged well, looking like an old mangy mutt left out in the rain after being beaten within an inch of his life with a wire hanger for pissing on the middle of the living room. His brown, matted and dirty hair was held back by a thick rubber band with skulls drawn with an ink pen. His eyes were sunken and bloodshot, as if he'd spent the night before on a binge, but danger still lurked there. I wouldn't be a bit surprised at some of the despicable acts he committed in his time on this world.

"Jack Phipps," he said, clumping to me in thick steel-toed boots. To my surprise, he held out one of his scarred, gargantuan hands. I was stunned for a moment, but found no recourse other than to shake it.

"It's been a long time, Renny," I said, fighting the urge to wince at the strength of his grip. I don't know if he exerted an inordinate amount of pressure on purpose or if he was caught in the emotion of a reunion. Of course, I went with the former despite his offering.

"You two know each other?" Mindy asked, darting her eyes between the two of us and trying to make the connection.

"Junior high and high school," I said. "Renny used to terrorize me."

Renny laughed loud and hard, but I caught a flash of anger in his eyes. I've been a pretty good judge of character, and I'm a firm believer people can change. But, I'd lay next month's rent Renny Hanks still hated the fact I still breathed, despite the little show he put on.

"So, you working here now, Big Jack?" he asked.

"Been here awhile. You must have just started."

"Last week. Came over from Milligan's. Used to run a press just like this sucker here. Of course, we didn't have no *safety engineer* to screw it up with a lot of worthless guarding."

"Renny, we've been down this road before," Mindy said. "OSHA isn't going to leave us with much of a choice. We have to do something, and I need your help to do it right. All the other operators have signed off on the guarding."

Renny liked the idea his help was required, and for the next hour, I worked side by side with my arch nemesis, stealing sideways glances at him to make sure he didn't clock me over the head with a pipe wrench. He caught my eye a couple of times and winked, though there wasn't an ounce of humor in his eyes.

We finished with the machine guarding assignment and thanked Renny for his time. Mindy and I walked back up the main factory aisle in silence. She shot a look over her shoulder to make sure nobody was within earshot.

"You actually went to school with him?" she asked.

"Surprised?"

"That he went to school?" she said. "Yeah."

Renny played Mr. Friendly for a couple of weeks, but the leopard hadn't changed a single spot. The day after maintenance installed the machine guarding, Mindy and I walked out to the parking lot together after work and found all four tires on both our cars flattened. Luckily, the surveillance video caught quite a nice image of Renny's mug punching them with a screwdriver. Management fired him on the spot, and the police arrested him for vandalism. They also caught him with several nice chunks of crystal meth in his pocket and sent him to County for two years for distribution. I was glad the sole cost of our reunion was four semi-bald tires.

The holidays came and went without much ado. I received some nice domestic gifts from my folks for the apartment and a twelve pack of Milwaukee's Best from Jake. Hey, it's the thought that counts, right? I spent my vacation days at the movies seeing the stellar bomb *Encino Man,* and the disturbing *Crying Game* with Mike and Stacy which sent Mike and I screaming from the theater at the end. The rest of the holiday vacation, I relaxed in my cozy little apartment and played Sonic the Hedgehog on my present to myself, a Sega Genesis system.

I had to admit I was lonely. Work was too busy in the fall to even think about getting a relationship going, but as I lay alone in a two-bedroom apartment, taking my use 'em or lose 'em vacation days, I found my mind drifting more and more to Diane. I went through my scrapbook several times, fingering pictures of the two of us over the years, grinning at the good times and the bad. But, I often returned to the picture she gave me those years ago at the fateful bra Christmas.

I ran my finger across the piece of paper I'd taped to the frame. Mike gave it to me in my hand-delivered wedding announcement. It was an address and phone number in Garden City, Kansas. He didn't put a name on it, but I didn't have to ask.

I must have picked up the phone a dozen times and dialed the number except for the last digit. For some reason, I couldn't bring myself to do it. I was terrified I wouldn't have anything to say past hello. Each time, I hung up the receiver and walked to the sliding glass door leading out to my little balcony over the lake. A petite, snow-covered gazebo balanced alongside the lake, reminding me of a little shack by a little stream in Nebraska.

I stared at the gazebo, and the phone beckoned me to dial her last stupid digit. If she asked me to come, I'd hop in the car in a heartbeat and drive the eight hours across the State of Kansas in record time. But, I couldn't get over the fear the request wouldn't come.

CHAPTER THIRTY-SIX

As a general rule, I hate weddings. The only reason I ever go is out of obligation by some familial relationship or if I haven't gotten a good fix of white wedding cake. Catholic weddings are the worst with the up and down motions, and Lutheran affairs don't rank much higher. Over the years, I came to prefer a good United Methodist wedding. They were quick, to the point and allowed people to get to the reception in a respectable timeframe.

On April 10, 1993, I stood in the bathroom of the United Methodist Church of the Resurrection, trying without success to fix the tie on my best friend's tux. His nervous hands shook too much to do the task himself. Mike maintained the picture of composure through the wedding planning process and didn't utter a word of doubt with the exception of the bachelor party night. But, with the music blaring from the strip club, I couldn't tell if he asked me why he was *doing* this, meaning the wedding, or why he *did* this, meaning drink fifteen Jell-O shots being offered by the big-breasted waitress.

"Tell me I'm doing the right thing, Jack," he said, eyes studying the bathroom ceiling.

"You're doing the right thing, Mike."

"Do you mean it?"

"Well, you asked me to say it. I'm trying to be a good best man."

I got the last crease out of his bowtie and clapped him on both shoulders. I checked my own image in the mirror. My hair started to thin up top, but I could still pass muster in a monkey suit.

"You're right," he said after a moment. "She's the one."

"You know it. Besides, I'm the one who should be quaking in my boots right now."

"Diane's here, you know. I saw her walking across the parking lot a half hour ago."

"How's she look?" I asked.

"Awesome, as usual."

I'd prepared myself for the chance I might run into Diane again. I even hit the gym to work off some of the winter weight which settled around my mid-section. My motivation was to ensure I looked better than any schmuck she might happen to bring along, and while I hoped she came alone, I wasn't counting on it. If Zack Hunter strolled up the aisle with her on his arm, I'd have to walk out of the chapel in the middle of the ceremony.

A tiny, red-faced man with tufts of white hair sprouting from his jowls stuck his head in the bathroom and told us it was time to start. Mike and I headed toward the back of the church where we'd hide in the choir room like cowering mice until it was time for us to stroll out. A couple of our fraternity brothers made the groomsmen list along with a guy I didn't know well from Mike's job. Like Mike, he was a psychologist at the hospital.

The organist nodded, and we walked out to the crowded sanctuary where the pastor awaited our arrival, a smile stretched on his round, thin face. The sanctuary was full, but Stacy's side outweighed Mike's.

"Last chance to back out," I whispered to Mike.

"Too late now. There's Diane, by the way, fifth pew from the front on the aisle. Don't trip and fall trying to find her."

My heart thundered in my chest, forcing a rush of blood which made my extremities tingle. I hoped I didn't end up on *America's Funniest Home Videos* by passing out and collapsing the entire row of pews on the bride's side of the aisle. I forced myself to wait until we locked in position before I tried to find Diane.

I studied my shiny black shoes for a moment, took a deep breath and raised my eyes. I found her within seconds, and the butterflies lying dormant in my stomach leapt forth with such veracity I was surprised a slew of the damn things didn't flutter out of my mouth. There she was, locking eyes with me and throwing a little wave she knew I couldn't return. There wasn't a man on either side of her, either.

I'd spent the last few months wondering how she'd look after a little over two years apart. Some images came up wonderful and some pictured her in a chunky dress with flabby arms gathering mounds of Twinkies and Ding Dongs into her mouth. But, the latter happened when I thought back to some of the darker times.

I don't know if she was the prime example of the old adage "absence makes the heart grow fonder," but she looked more ravishing than ever. Her long, dark hair was replaced by a stylish chopped cut accentuating her high cheekbones and a more unimpeded view of her beautiful face. I must have looked like a moron as I wondered why I didn't touch base with her. I thought I was over Diane Riven, but at that moment, I realized I never stopped loving her.

The wedding went off without a hitch, though I almost dropped the rings. The pastor made an expert grab before they could hit the floor. I was so consumed with Diane during the wedding itself he could have given the sermon in Yiddish, and I wouldn't have known any better.

The reception was held at the Brookridge Country Club, a nice, private golf course with a spacious clubhouse off 103rd Street in Overland Park. I stayed behind at the church and took fourteen million pictures with the bridal party, and with each shutter snap, I cursed Mike he didn't schedule the pictures before the wedding. It took me an hour to shake loose, and I made a beeline to the country club.

Pulling into the parking lot twenty minutes later, I jogged to the front entrance. Bursting through the double doors, I clacked my way across the ceramic tile, heading back to the party, forcing myself to walk or I'd be rendered speechless by the time I found her. But, as hard as I scoured the room, I couldn't see Diane anywhere. My spirit crushed when I realized my little glimpse of her in the chapel might be all I got.

Ten minutes later, Mike and Stacy arrived with a boisterous announcement from the DJ. The crowd climbed to their feet from their circular tables and gave the obligatory applauds and whistles. After they cut the cake and drank champagne with their arms intertwined, it came time for the toast from the best man and bridesmaid. Stacy's friend Renee gave a heartfelt speech about their growing up together, and more than a couple of hands swiped at their eyes.

I had a well-crafted speech prepared, but my heart wasn't in it. Diane's absence crushed my spirits. However, I reminded myself tonight was for Mike and Stacy, not for my sorry behind. I walked over and took the outstretched microphone from the DJ, stepping on a little platform so I was visible to the crowd. I prayed they couldn't spy my shaking knees.

"Well, anybody who knew Mike growing up ever think we'd be here?" I asked. The crowd laughed and there were several resounding shouts of no. "But yet here we are, celebrating the joining of two lives. I tried to think of what I would say once I took the stage. I thought I'd be the one in the crowd with the ring, and Mike would be up here embarrassing me."

At the back of the crowd, Diane walked through the door. She stopped when she spotted me with the microphone in my hand and leaned against the doorway. God, she looked good.

"See, the thing is Mike is a smart man. Not only did he keep me as his best friend for all these years, he was smart enough to hold onto the best thing that ever happened to him, the former Miss Stacy Dunbrooke. Turns out he was smarter than I ever was. So, raise a glass and let's toast the happy couple. May your days ahead be full of wonder and joy. To the bride and groom."

Glasses clinked, Mike leaned in and kissed Stacy, and another round of applause erupted. The DJ played a slow song I didn't recognize, and the new couple broke their kiss and swayed to the music. I hopped from the podium, getting a pat on the back from my parents as I headed to the back. Diane walked forward to meet me.

"Hey, Diane," I said, my tongue as dry as a desert.

"Hi, Jack. Great toast."

The sight of her before me again rendered me speechless for a moment. I was surprised I could get her name out of my mouth without screwing it up.

I drank in her face. "You look absolutely fantastic."

"So do you. I thought about calling you so many times, but..."

She trailed off and dropped her eyes to the floor, unsure how to continue.

"I know. I think I dialed your number a thousand times, but couldn't bring myself to hit the last digit."

She raised her chin, the light in her blue eyes blazing. "See? We still think alike, even after this long."

"I think we're both idiots."

"I think you're right," she said, her laugh like a melody to my ears.

The DJ announced it was time for the bridal party to join in the dance.

"That's your cue," she said. I nodded and half-turned toward the dance floor.

"I know I'm supposed to dance with the maid of honor," I said. "But, I've never been much for tradition, and I don't think there's anyone on this planet I'd rather dance with than you."

There it was. I'd spread myself wide open, my feelings on my sleeve. I didn't know what she'd say and I was terrified. Would she say I'd better go dance with the maid of honor and we'd catch up later? Would she say she didn't think it was such a good idea? Would she say she'd like to but her boyfriend was waiting in the car? Instead of a negative response, she slid her hand in the crook of my arm and tugged me forward.

We walked to the dance floor, the smiles of those who knew our history apparent. I think I even saw my mom tear up. We swayed to the music, and as I pulled her a bit closer, her cheek rested against mine. It was absolute heaven.

"I missed you, Jack," she whispered. "I still miss you."

If someone offered me a million dollars to wipe the grin from my face at that moment, I would have told him to go take a long walk off a short pier because it was a losing proposition. I pulled her even tighter and we continued swaying to the music.

"I missed you too, Diane."

CHAPTER THIRTY-SEVEN

We got married on February 1, 1994 in the same church where Mike and Stacy were married. Once Diane and I were together again, and without the obligation we stay together because we'd been together for so long, our relationship reached a newer and deeper level. She never stopped loving me, and I didn't stop loving her. I think we needed the separation to realize we were destined to be together.

The wedding itself was a spectacular affair. Diane knocked my eyes out in a white gown, laced with sparkling beads and a train stretching to Oklahoma. Mike was my best man, and we threw a juicy but tasteful bachelor party. By bachelor party law, I am obligated to secrecy about the actual events, but suffice it to say we were good boys.

The lone awkward moment of the wedding occurred when it was time for the father of the bride to give his little girl away. Mr. Riven clamped a vise grip on Diane's arm, and I thought for a moment I would have to get Mike to fetch me a crow bar so we could pry him loose and get on with the ceremony. In the end, he let her go and handed her to me. As he placed her hand in mine, he even flashed a thin line of teeth under shimmering eyes.

"Take care of my little baby," he said. It was the first emotion he'd displayed other than contempt for me.

Diane found a job teaching first grade at a local elementary school. She was excited about her class with the exception of the Minor twins who she heard horror stories about from the kindergarten teachers and other mothers of children in her class.

Ecstatic to be back in Kansas City, Diane searched for a house for the two of us. We found a nice three-bedroom Cape Cod on a tree-filled lot a mile from my parents' house, which was both a good and bad thing. On the good side, they were close enough for me to borrow tools from my dad which was good because all I had were a hand saw, a hammer and a drill with a frayed cord. On the bad side, my mother found occasion to drop by unannounced at any time of the day or night to check how things were going. Diane, to her credit, didn't raise an eyebrow concerning my mom's visits.

We enjoyed our married life, as if our time apart made our relationship stronger. We exchanged tales of our lives during those two years apart, though hers was far more tumultuous than mine. She'd dated Zack for a year before she caught him cheating on her with an old girlfriend. She said I was right about him, a phrase I cherished when uttered because of its scarcity. Her father suffered a heart attack and retired to Michigan, spending his days fishing and playing golf. There was a scary stint with a stalker while Diane worked in Garden City, but the police caught the guy. He had enough warrants out for him that they put him away for a while for which I was thankful.

Luckily for us, life was much calmer in the suburbs during our first year of marriage. We relived a lot of great old memories and built the foundation for new ones. Marital spats were rare and even when they arose, we made quick amends in the bedroom.

We weren't quite sure, but we think it was an argument over getting a dog and the ensuing make-up session leading to our best surprise ever. Two weeks shy of our one-year anniversary, Diane told me she was pregnant. After the shock wore off, I gathered her in my arms, stroking her hair and kissing her neck. I thought our reunited moment on the dance floor was the happiest in my life, but I was wrong. The thought of a baby and Diane as its mother was such an enthralling thought it would have taken a belt sander to get the smile off my face.

We spent the next nine months in a frenzy, getting things ready for the baby. I opposed finding out the sex of the child with the utmost vehemence, though the uncertainty killed Diane.

"We've got to know," she said while we returned duplicate gifts from our baby shower. "How are we going to know what color to paint the room?"

"We'll paint it a neutral color," I said, reaching over and rubbing her protruding, round belly. It was a boy. I just knew it. Diane agreed, at least that's what she told me, though I knew she hoped for a little girl.

"I don't understand how you can stand not knowing," she said. The sonogram results were one of our few continuing debates.

"Honey, it's life's last great surprise. Think of the anticipation."

She pinched my arm. "I don't want anticipation, you twit. I want to know what freaking color to paint the baby's room."

We were ready to have the baby, weary of doctor's appointments, lab tests, satisfying late night cravings of ice cream, being clueless at parenting classes and I'm pretty sure I developed some sort of cumulative trauma disorder from giving daily backrubs.

Five weeks later, Diane poked me awake from a dead sleep. I dreamed I was back on the campus of K-State running through Durland Hall trying to find room A203 for my Physics final. However, there wasn't an A in front of any of the room numbers and 203 was full of naked midgets in black aprons working on engine blocks. Diane's pokes at my arms woke me, and I wondered what I'd eaten to make me dream that monstrosity.

"It's time," she said, leaning over my shoulder. I raised my head and deciphered the blurred red digits of the clock—5:30 AM.

"Honey, I don't have to get up for another half hour." I plopped my head back to my pillow, hoping I wouldn't fall back into the midget dream again.

She poked again, firmer this time. "No, Jack, it's *time*."

I lurched with a start, wide-awake. Diane raised her eyebrows and held her belly tight. Wetness grew against my hip, and I realized her water broke. I was going to be a father.

CHAPTER THIRTY-EIGHT

There are no words to describe the joy of witnessing your child being born into this world. Until that moment in time, I thought the reunion at Mike's wedding and our own nuptials were the happiest moments in my life, but they didn't hold a candle to setting eyes on my child for the first time.

We stormed the hospital just after six in the morning after scrambling around trying to find the duffel bag we'd put together for this occasion. It was in the exact spot I meant to put it, but my brain ran haywire and it took a good twenty minutes of tearing through closets and cabinets trying to find it. As we rolled out the door, clothes lay scattered and furniture turned aside as if a pack of invading barbarians ransacked our home.

We'd pre-filled most of the paperwork to expedite the registration process and they placed Diane in a room. I made quick phone calls to my folks and my brother and to her parents in Michigan. They promised to get to Kansas City as quick as possible. I hoped for Diane's sake they made it before the baby came.

The hands of the clock in our room creaked as the next ten hours dragged at a snail's pace with a flurry of doctors and nurses coming and going. The labor pains drew closer, and the doc estimated we'd be good to go in an hour or two. My folks marked time in the waiting room with Mike and Stacy who ventured over since we were close to go time.

Diane's parents arrived in hour number twelve after getting stuck on the ground in Detroit waiting for a mechanic to fix a light on the left wing of the plane. They were ecstatic they didn't miss the main event, and Mr. Riven even patted me on the back and asked how was holding up. Another contraction struck, and Diane screamed something unintelligible at me. It must have been a bad one, because I think she gave me stress fractures in my right hand.

Diane's eyes betrayed her exhaustion as I wiped the beading sweat off her forehead. I rubbed ice chips on her cracked lips and kissed her temple.

"You doing okay, honey?" I asked.

"What the hell do you think?" She screamed as another contraction hit. I suppose I deserved that. Ask a stupid question, get a barb shot back at you.

"We're really, really close, babe. Just hang on."

"Easy for you to say, Jack," she said, gasping, sweat beading on her brow. "Try pushing a bowling ball out of your belly button and tell me how close is close enough."

She crushed my hand as another contraction swept over her, and I winced at the fracture growing with each successive squeeze. The doc came in and assumed the catcher's position, telling Diane to breathe and push. Diane screamed loud enough to shake the glassware in the room, and I was quite surprised some of it didn't shatter into a million pieces. In addition to the cap and gown they give to the father-to-be, I think a standard set of earplugs would be in order.

When the top of the baby's head poked through, I nearly

forgot Diane, wanting to go to the doctor and help him bring my child forth. But, Diane's vice grip on my now throbbing right hand would have prevented any such maneuver even if I'd tried. The doc asked for a big push, and Diane screeched again, succeeding in getting the baby's shoulders clear. With that barrier overcame, my child slid right out, and what we created lay before me.

"It's a boy," the doctor said. "A beautiful baby boy."

Diane cried with joy, and I couldn't hold back my emotions any longer. I leaned over and hugged and kissed her and told her how much I loved her, my happy tears mingling with her own. The nurses cleaned our son and placed him in Diane's outstretched arms. His brown eyes were wide and searching, his brow furrowed, no doubt wondering what happened to his cozy home and who these people were crying over him. Diane kissed his head.

"He's beautiful, Jack," she said.

Now, I've seen my share of newborn pictures in my time, and I've yet to spot one resembling anything other than a scrunched, red lizard. But, my little boy was the exception, and I knew we'd be getting calls from Johnson & Johnson and Gerber wanting to put our boy's pictures in their ads. With a face like his, he'd generate millions of dollars in revenue.

"He looks like his mother," I said, kissing her again. Diane's eyes shimmered.

"William?" she asked.

William was the name we pretty much agreed on for a boy. I was reluctant because we went to junior high with William Younders, an obnoxious little twerp we called Weird Willy. There were plenty of other Wills and Bills who were fine, outstanding citizens of this country, but the connotation the name William raised wasn't positive for me. However, William was also the name of Diane's grandfather to whom she was close and who passed away six months earlier from a stroke. I couldn't think of a better request of my wife to honor.

"William it is," I said. "I'd better go spill the good news before they break the door."

I ventured into the hallway and am pretty sure I floated along the linoleum. A boy. I had a baby boy. Great visions of him flashed through my brain. Valedictorian, Captain of the baseball team, Heisman Trophy winner, Rhodes Scholar…all things within reach.

When I made the announcement to the waiting crowd, I don't think there was a dry eye in the house. Even Jake, the proud uncle, turned away for a second to draw an arm across his face. Mike swept me off the ground in a bear hug. He whipped out cigars and passed them to the boys in the room and even a couple of guys who happened to be walking by. I hate cigars, but I still have the memento in a drawer in my dresser on top of Will's birth certificate.

The rest of the day was a blur with family and friends and co-workers rotating in and out of our room. Diane was exhausted and tried to catnap in between knocks on the door. With visiting hours over, the foot traffic died, and it was me, my wife and our sleeping son, swaddled tight in a blue and white blanket. Diane dozed off without the threat of someone else coming in to wake her up. I walked to her bed and plucked Will from her arms. I carried him across the room and settled in the rocking chair, swaying back and forth, watching my son with wide-eyed wonderment.

Out the window, the summer sun slipped below the horizon, setting the skyline ablaze with a wondrous barrage of orange and red. It was the most peaceful moment of my life, and I was the luckiest man in the world.

CHAPTER THIRTY-NINE

I tried hard but couldn't come up with a more life-changing experience than having a baby. Those couples without children may think they know what they're getting themselves into, but they haven't a clue. I don't care how much they love children or how many times they've babysat their nieces and nephews. Until you have to wake up three or four times a night to feed and change the baby, your brain whirring about their well-being, you can't imagine the demands an infant puts on your body and soul. For the first six months, I was in a perpetual fog—failing to get a sufficient amount of sleep to function beyond meeting my body and job's most basic demands.

By the same token, it was the most wonderful experience of my life. Watching Will's little mind work to assimilate the world around him was awesome. My kid's toothless grin and cute little gurgle would turn even the stormiest of days into a perpetual sunny sky. It was those memories keeping you going when you're wiping sticky crap off little bird legs at 3 AM just as you fell into a deep and relaxing sleep from the last round.

I blinked and it was Will's first birthday party. The family gathered around the table, sang happy birthday and watched him get more birthday cake in his hair and on his clothes than in his mouth. Diane took a year off school and stayed home with him. I took a day off work every so often and bought her a full body massage at her favorite salon to keep her sanity.

By Will's second birthday, Mike and Stacy decided they'd done enough traveling to Rio, Europe, Aruba and some little known island in the South Pacific where they scuba dove for a week. It was time to make a baby of their own, and in June 1996, little Alex Washington was born to the world. Mike beamed at the prospect of being a dad, and I realized how much he'd grown since college.

In 1997, my dad made the decision to retire from the construction business and become a full-time grandfather, in between fishing expeditions and trips with my mom. My folks didn't travel much over the years, always saving money for the rainy day that failed to come. You noticed the ever-present weight of the world slip from my dad's shoulders when in near proximity to Little Will. My dad was a great father, but each visit reminded me how different he was from the man who brought me up. He wantonly gave Will money for his piggy bank or a piece of candy he carried around in his pocket. I needed a written and notarized Executive Order from the President to get either when I grew up. Now, it seems he gave out the stash he'd been saving over the last two decades.

Will, in the meantime, suckered both Diane and I. He skipped his terrible two's and saved his terror and mayhem for his third year. We called him Will the Destructor—he destroyed anything he could lay his hands on. New leather sofa? Permanent marker he'd scaled the counters to get to. Our decks of playing cards? Mangled, bent and chewed. Actually, that one worked out pretty well on poker night for me. Our carpet? A rainbow of mashed in Play-Dough you couldn't quite get out—even with the wonderous new OxyClean. It was tough to get mad at him because he'd grin at you, daring you to punish him and he was so damned cute doing it.

We lost a few pets along the way. A hamster named George disappeared from his cage one sunny spring afternoon and was never seen again. A parakeet named Quincy plummeted to the bottom of his cage on an icy weekday morning. Will took those with surprising calmness and a mature sense of the circle of life. However, when Thundar the Turtle plodded to the big shell in the sky, Will lost it for days. Perhaps because he was the one who "saved" Thundar from drowning in a creek where we'd gone fishing one afternoon. Diane ended up saving the day, as she always did, by burying Thundar in our backyard and putting a picture of Will and the turtle on the grave.

"Can he see it, Momma?" Will asked.

"Sure, honey," she said. "Now Thundar will have you next to him and you'll always be together."

Little Will squatted at the tiny gravesite, straightening the wooded cross he'd made and tilting the picture so it was just right. Comforted for the first in days, he hugged his mom and ran off toward the swing set.

Things were on cruise control for my little family. I'd watch the news and hear the horrific things going on around the world and in our own city. It was an exercise in depression to watch the news. When one of those stories would come across the screen, I'd sweep my eyes across my beautiful wife and son playing on the floor and remember how good I had it. But, I'd taken enough physics in my college days to know how nature works, that what goes up, must eventually come down.

On a chilly afternoon in late September 1996, I raked leaves in the backyard. Our neighborhood was old with mature trees shedding leaves the size of surfboards. We lived in a house on the corner, and the fall winds blew most of the neighborhood's leaves into my yard. I'd already accumulated eighteen large plastic trash bags full of the little buggers, and I knew I'd have to hit up Timmy Moss down the street for another roll to help out his Boy Scout troop.

For every pile I raked, Will ran with a full head of steam and dove into them, sending at least half of them flying into the cool breeze. At least some of them went over the fence into my neighbor's yard, but it still made more work for me.

"Mom," I said toward the porch. "Control your grandson, will you?"

Wrapped in a worn, red wool coat and drinking a cup of coffee, she smiled and waved, ignoring my request. She would do nothing but let her little angel wreak all the havoc he wanted. My dad was inside, glued to the television watching the O.J. Simpson trial, certain his once favorite football star would get convicted of murdering his wife and her "friend."

With her coat on, Diane stuck her head out the front door. She was in the middle of making dinner, and I sensed a run to the store in my future. Jake was bringing his steady girlfriend to meet the family. According to him, she was "the one." Mom liked her, which is more than I can say of any of the other skanks he brought home in his day.

"Honey," she said. "I need milk for the potatoes. I'm going to run to the store."

"Do you want me to go?" I half-hoped she'd say no.

"Don't worry about it, I'll be right back."

She disappeared back into the house, and Will crashed into my leg, catching me off balance and sending me falling into the pile of leaves I'd just finished gathering. I'm lucky the rake didn't hit me anyplace special. My mom laughed as Will and I steamrolled through the pile. I picked up my giggling son and tossed him in the air. My mom walked to my side.

"Getting quite a workout from this little guy," she said.

"He's a handful. You still watching him tomorrow night? Diane and I have that charity deal to go to."

She took him from me and kissed his neck until he giggled and squirmed. Will thought the sun shone through Grandma's navel. She didn't have the chance to answer my question. Our conversation was interrupted by a car horn, a squeal of tires and a thunderous sound of metal meeting metal. My blood ran cold as my brain ran through a quick calculation of the time it would have taken Diane to get her keys, back out of the driveway and cross the busy intersection at our corner.

"Oh, no," I whispered. "Call 911, Mom."

I threw the rake and sprinted to the back gate. A scream erupted from our corner, and by the time I cleared the hedge running along the street, I already knew what happened.

Diane's mini-van lay crushed on its top, smoke emanating from the hood and tires still spinning from the impact. Several feet away the crumpled front end of a 1980's style black Trans-Am smoked, a dead ringer for the one Burt Reynold's drove in Smokey and the Bandit. A tattooed man with a ragged blonde mullet and sleeveless shirt attempted to climb out of the driver's side door, blood pouring from a nasty gash on his forehead. He staggered for a couple of feet before collapsing to an awkward sitting position on the street. A woman walking a large golden retriever across the street was the one doing the screaming.

I ran as fast as my wobbling legs would carry me to the opposite side of our mini-van, the tears already forming with worry. I dropped to the ground, ignoring the broken glass biting into my hands and legs. Diane was still buckled in, eyes glassy and dazed. Blood from multiple lacerations on her chin and forehead carved lines in her pretty face. I tried opening the door, but the impact rammed it shut.

"Diane," I said, trying to remain calm and take the fear out of my voice. "Diane, can you hear me?"

She tried to turn her head, but winced with pain. Instead, she ticked her head.

"Can't breathe," she said, wheezing. "Seatbelt."

I didn't know what I should do. I was afraid to move her even if I could get the crushed door open. I also didn't want her to hang with the seatbelt crushing her lungs. Gasoline spread along the ground toward the smoking engine, and I had to get her out. A bald man with a striking resemblance to Mr. Clean jogged up and helped me with the car door. With several labored tugs, it screeched open.

"Sweetie," I said, "I'm going to undo your seatbelt and we're going to get you out of here. The ambulance is on the way."

"Oh God," she said, tears streaming, her body shaking. "I'm scared."

I reached across her, having Mr. Clean help support her upper body as I undid her seatbelt. She slipped into our arms, and we carried her to the curb. Supporting her head in my lap, my head swung around for any sign of professional help. The sirens in the distance wailed, drawing closer.

"Jack?" Diane said, her voice a cracked whisper. Her eyes shimmered with fearful tears as I stroked her blood-matted hair.

"What baby?"

"Tell me I'm going to be okay. Tell me everything is going to be fine, because you have never lied to me and I'll believe you."

It was true I hadn't lied to her, not once in our time together. But, as the legs of my jeans grew wetter, I reached behind her head and found it soaked with blood. Hot tears flowed, but I tried to keep a brave face.

"You're going to be fine, Diane. Just fine."

She crinkled her eyes at me. "Liar." She erupted into a coughing fit, blood spraying in a fine mist from her mouth. I was so damned scared and helpless I wanted to scream. When the coughing subsided, she turned to me again. "You are the best thing that ever happened to me, Jack Phipps. Take care of Will."

"Don't talk like that," I said, already noticing her fade before my eyes.

"I love you," she said, three little words before the light in her eyes disappeared. As I held her and screamed and cried, the police and ambulance arrived in a mess of sirens and whirring lights, but it was too late. My baby was gone.

I don't remember much about the hours after the accident. I went after the drunk who killed her, but the police held me back. He registered a .22 blood alcohol concentration and sped 75 miles per hour on a 25 mile per hour street. He killed my wife with his stupidity, and the sole injury to his drunken frame was a cut on his forehead. The judge gave him fifteen years in prison for driving under the influence, his fifth offense, and for vehicular manslaughter.

The worst part was telling Will his mommy wouldn't be coming home anymore. At three, he didn't understand, but his grief was enormous. I braced myself over the next several months for the hurricane to hit, but he remained quiet, the two of us settling into something of a routine.

"I want to see Mommy," he said one morning, adorned in his pajamas and watching Scooby Doo from my lap.

"I do to, buddy. I wish we could."

"No," he said. "I want to go see her rock."

It took a minute before it registered he wanted to go to her grave. We got dressed and headed to the cemetery. I don't know what brought on his sudden urge to visit Diane's grave, but if it would help him with the grieving process, I was for it. Who knew, it might help me as well.

Cars scattered along the narrow driveway of the cemetery, folks stationed at various points visiting with their dearly departed. Diane's grave rested in the northwest corner of the cemetery, higher than the other gravesites under a large oak tree. Will and I climbed out of the car, and I let him lead the way.

I ground my teeth to fight the looming tears as I listened to my son tell his mom the wonderful things going on in his life—pre-school, friends, his favorite cartoons. Hearing his high voice choking with emotion about killed me.

"I miss you, Mommy and I love you," he said. He pulled something from his jacket and squatted in front of her tombstone. He wiped his eyes on the sleeve of his coat before grabbing onto me. I scooped him up and held him as tight as I could. He didn't cry any more, but gripped my neck as if he was terrified I would disappear too. Over his shoulder, at the base of the tombstone, he placed a picture of him and Diane, cheek-to-cheek, smiling, loving each other. A picture for her. A picture so they would always be together.

I was devastated, subject to frequent and uncontrollable crying fits over the next several months. I tried to find a way to deal with the grief and the rage inside me. I don't know if I would have made without the little boy who needed me. Will was my savior and carried me through the darkest moment I hope I ever have to live through.

His questions would come and I struggled with how to answer them. I tried to be as strong as possible for him and keep the memory of his mother alive. We visited her grave each month and put fresh flowers on the mound. I gave him some time alone to talk to her. Sometimes he would say nothing and stand at her tombstone. Sometimes he would talk for several minutes about things going on at school or Grandma or Grandpa. He didn't ask why the picture was gone—I think he assumed Diane took it herself.

I decided at last when he did ask, I would tell him the whole story—our story. I would tell him not how his mother died, but rather how she lived. I think Diane would have wanted it that way.

EPILOGUE

The winds grew icy and biting, and the leaves long since departed from the trees. The branches I didn't find the time or energy to trim scraped in protest against window panes on the second floor where Will and I sat. He wanted to know about his mom, and I was as truthful as I could be in telling him the tale of our lives. His light, seven-year-old body perched on my lap, and his ever-inquisitive mind broke its silent bonds for the first time in hours.

"It happened right there?" He pointed out to the intersection where Diane was killed.

"Right there." I tried to avoid sounding as broken as my spirit. Though her death was over four years ago, my trip down memory lane with Will scraped scabs from wounds which never quite healed.

"Are you okay, Dad?"

"Yeah, buddy. I'm fine."

"Do you want to hold Rolf?" he asked, holding out his stuffed dog.

I rubbed his head. "No thanks. You hold onto Rolf."

"You know, I'm really too old to have a stuffed dog," he said, stroking the top of Rolf's well-worn head.

"To be honest with you, champ, I don't think you're ever

too old."

Will fell silent once again and gazed out the window. I didn't know what rolled through his young mind. I didn't know to what degree he remembered his mother. He kept a picture of her on his nightstand and said goodnight to her. Most nights, it was a simple detail, as much a pattern as brushing your teeth before bedtime. Every once in a while, though, he'd say his goodnight to her picture as his little fingers traced the outline of her face. I'd watch him from the doorway, wondering if he'd picked up the habit from me.

As we watched from the window, a large moving van rolled through the pile of leaves and backed into the driveway of the Swinson house across the street—Diane's old house. The Swinson's moved somewhere in the northeast, perhaps into Maine. His friend, Tommy, had been part of the Swinson clan, and Will moped for a month after they left. Now someone else rolled into the neighborhood to take their place—the suburban circle of life.

Will climbed to his knees and pressed his hands and nose against the cold glass, his hot breath fogging his reflection. A new Chevy Blazer pulled to the curb in front of the house, and a young family emerged. The father was a lanky fellow who stretched his gangly limbs as he spun full circle to check out the new neighborhood. A pretty red-head popped out the passenger side and did the same visual exploration before opening the back door.

"Whoa," Will said, his chestnut eyes wide at what came out.

She was about eight years old with beautiful long red hair pulled into a ponytail. As if on cue, she looked across the street and to the second floor where we watched and she waved. Thank goodness my son was smarter than his old man because he waved back.

"Can I go over there, Dad?"

"Sure, buddy. Watch the street."

I stayed where I was and observed the movers unload the appliances. The father and mother pulled boxes out of the back of the Blazer and carried them inside. The little girl stood on the front walk by the door, and a sense of déjà vu swept over me, strong enough to bowl me over. I wondered if my son would be able to grasp the similarity of today and twenty-two years ago.

Will appeared by the bedroom door. He wore his good jacket, and a brush somehow wove its way through his usual bird's nest. "Hey, Dad. Wouldn't it be kinda cool if her name was Diane?"

Tears welled in my eyes, and a lump the size of a small boulder lodged itself in my throat. Unable to speak, I nodded in affirmation. Will smiled and ran downstairs and out the front door. I watched the two close the distance between them, shake hands and begin to talk. As they talked, it began to snow, large fluttering flakes swaying back and forth in the breeze as they floated to earth. A blanket of white on its way to wash away the pain and let those bound by the past begin life anew.

Thanks, Diane.

THE END